Here

Two people move into an emp[...] life together. Should the bed g[...] there and the table here? Everything inside this small space is for them to decide. The responsibility is daunting – particularly when they reflect that it has taken the whole history of the world to get them together in this particular place at this particular time; and that the whole future of the world will be different if the table is here instead of there. But how to decide *anything*, when the other person keeps disagreeing with you, and when the woman downstairs maddeningly dumps unwanted items of furniture on you that you haven't the heart to refuse . . .?

Michael Frayn was born in 1933 in the suburbs of London. He began his career as a reporter on the *Guardian,* then became a columnist, first for the *Guardian* and then for the *Observer*. A selection of his columns has been included in *The Original Michael Frayn,* (Methuen, 1990). He has written eight novels: *The Tin Men, The Russian Interpreter, Towards the End of the Morning, A Very Private Life, Sweet Dreams, The Trick of It, A Landing on the Sun* and *Now You Know,* together with a volume of philosophy, *Constructions*. He has written two original screenplays – one for the cinema, *Clockwise,* and one for television, *First and Last,* and nine plays for the stage, including: *Alphabetical Order, Donkeys' Years, Clouds, Make and Break, Noises Off, Benefactors* and *Look Look*. He has translated Chekhov's last four plays, dramatised a selection of his one-act plays and short stories under the title of *The Sneeze* and adapted his first, untitled play, as *Wild Honey*. He has also translated one modern Russian play – Yuri Trifonov's *Exchange*. All his plays and translations have been published by Methuen.

MICHAEL FRAYN

HERE

a play in two acts

METHUEN DRAMA

METHUEN MODERN PLAYS

First published in Great Britain 1993
by Methuen Drama
an imprint of Reed Consumer Books Ltd
Michelin House, 81 Fulham Road, London SW3 6RB
and Auckland, Melbourne, Singapore and Toronto

ISBN 0-413-68130-0

A CIP catalogue record for this book
is available at the British Library

Typeset by Hewer Text Composition Services, Edinburgh
Printed in Great Britain by Cox & Wyman Ltd, Reading, Berkshire

Front cover image by Slatter Anderson

HERE

Here was first presented at the Donmar Warehouse Theatre, by arrangement with Michael Codron, on Thursday 29 July 1993, with the following cast:

CATH   Teresa Banham
PHIL   Iain Glen
PAT   Brenda Bruce

Directed by Michael Blakemore
Designed by Ashley Martin-Davis
Lighting Designed by Mark Henderson

ACT ONE

An empty room.

Two doors. Window. Bare floor, bare walls, no furniture. A kitchenette cupboard, shelves, and an alcove with a curtain, now pulled back to reveal a rail with a few wire coat-hangers on it.

Scene One

One of the doors is unlocked and pushed open. On the threshold stands CATH, holding the key on a label. She comes cautiously into the room, followed by PHIL. They look dubiously around.

CATH. No?

PHIL. No. No?

CATH. No.

PHIL goes out. CATH takes a last look round. He reappears.

PHIL. What?

CATH. Nothing.

They both look round.

PHIL. You mean . . .?

CATH. No . . . No!

She goes out. He continues to look around the room.

PHIL. No.

He turns to go. She reappears.

CATH. Not unless you . . .?

PHIL. Me? No. Not if you . . .

CATH. No . . .

She looks round the room.

PHIL. I mean, what do you think?

CATH. I don't know . . .

PHIL. Oh, I see.

CATH. No, no – if you think no . . .

PHIL. Yes, but I want to know what *you* think.

CATH. I think you think no.

PHIL. You mean you *don't* think no?

CATH. I just think . . . I don't know . . .

PHIL. You don't think *yes*? You're not saying you think *yes*?

CATH. No! No.

PHIL. But you don't think no?

CATH. No, but I know *you* think no.

PHIL. Not at all.

CATH. You *don't* think no?

PHIL. Not if *you* don't think no.

CATH. No, well . . .

They move about the room, looking. She opens the kitchenette.

PHIL. What?

CATH. The cooker's a bit . . .

PHIL. Yes.

She closes it. He opens the second door.

So's the bath.

She looks as well.

CATH. Yes . . .

He closes it. She pulls the curtain across to close off the alcove.

Not very . . .

PHIL. Not very.

She draws the curtain back again. He looks out of the window.

CATH. What?

PHIL. Nothing.

CATH. The view?

She joins him at the window. They look out.

Well . . .

PHIL. Fine.

CATH. Reasonably.

PHIL. Absolutely.

CATH. Isn't it?

PHIL. Yes. Yes!

They move about the room again.

I just think it's all a bit . . . I don't know . . . A bit . . .

CATH. I see what you mean . . .

PHIL. Don't *you* find it a bit . . . I mean, just a bit?

CATH. I suppose so.

PHIL. You don't.

CATH. No, I do. I do.

PHIL. We are both saying what we really think?

CATH *I'm* saying what I really think.

PHIL. I can't bear it when we just say what we think each other thinks.

CATH. You mean when I do.

PHIL. When either of us does.

CATH. Yes.

PHIL. I'm not getting at *you*.

CATH. No.

PHIL. I'm just saying, if we don't know what each other actually
thinks . . .

CATH. I know.

PHIL. But you really do think . . .?

CATH. Yes! Yes!

PHIL. You mean, that it's a bit . . .?

CATH. A bit.

PHIL. Yes . . .

Pause.

A bit what?

CATH. What?

PHIL. I'm not absolutely clear what you mean.

CATH. I mean it's a bit . . . well . . .

PHIL. Whatever?

CATH. Yes . . . All the same . . .

PHIL. Ah.

CATH. No.

PHIL. Go on.

CATH. Nothing.

PHIL. No, say it, say it.

CATH. Well . . . I don't know . . .

Pause.

We could put the bed *here*.

PHIL. Oh. So you're saying . . .?

CATH. I'm not saying anything. I'm just saying we could put the bed here.

PHIL. I see.

CATH. What?

PHIL. Nothing.

CATH. Or there. That's all I'm saying. The bed could go there. Or here. In which case the table could go here.

PHIL. Yes. Well.

CATH. What?

PHIL. I think we need to think about this.

CATH. We *are* thinking about it.

PHIL. We *are* thinking about it?

CATH. Aren't we?

PHIL. What – seriously *thinking* about it?

CATH. Not *seriously* thinking about it. Just thinking about it . . .

PHIL. Just thinking about it. All right.

CATH. No?

PHIL. Fine.

CATH. You *said* – we ought to think about it!

PHIL. I mean go away and think about it.

CATH. Go *away* and think about it?

PHIL. Cath, we were walking down the street. Yes?

CATH. Yes . . . What street? Which street?

PHIL. What street? Which street? This street! Five minutes ago. Right? Just walking down the street, talking about . . . I don't know . . .

CATH. The other place.

PHIL. What other place?

CATH. The other place we're thinking about.

PHIL. What other place we're thinking about?

CATH. What do you mean, what other place we're thinking about?

PHIL. Oh, you mean . . .?

CATH. Yes! That's what we were talking about!

PHIL. I thought we *weren't* thinking about that one?

CATH. I thought we were?

PHIL. Yes, well, anyway, never mind that . . .

CATH. No, only that's what we were talking about . . .

PHIL. Right.

CATH. I'm not trying to, you know . . .

PHIL. I know, I know. But the point is, we were walking down the street. We saw the board. We rang the bell . . . And that was five minutes ago! We didn't even know this place existed.

CATH. No, but now we do.

PHIL. Now we do, yes, and all I'm saying is, it's something we can begin to think about.

CATH. Yes . . .

PHIL. Cath, we're talking about something we're going to be looking at every single day of our lives. That's what we're deciding.

CATH. I know.

PHIL. Not just one quick look – how does it seem? – fine – right, get the sandwiches out. We're not talking about a picnic-place.

CATH. I know.

PHIL. We're talking about every day, day in, day out, for years and years to come. We're talking about lying here . . . yes?

CATH. Or here.

PHIL. Or here, yes, and waking up every morning, and seeing . . .
this. Right? These walls.

CATH. Yes.

PHIL. This floor, this ceiling.

CATH. Yes.

PHIL *This*.

CATH. I know.

PHIL. Every morning. Seven times a week. Thirty times a month.
Three hundred and sixty-five times a year.

CATH. We'd be away sometimes.

PHIL. And that's just for starters! We get up, we make breakfast,
we sit here. What do we see?

CATH. This.

PHIL. We have lunch, we have dinner. We read. We work. We talk
to each other. And what do we see?

CATH. We see this.

PHIL. Minute after minute. Hour after hour. We go to bed.

CATH. Still this.

PHIL. Wake up next morning . . .

CATH. We'd get used to it.

PHIL. Right. Exactly! We'd get used to it. That's what I'm saying.
Is this what we want to get used to?

CATH. But if it wasn't *this* room it would be somewhere else!

PHIL. Yes, but it *would* be this room! That's my point! Do you see?

CATH. Well . . .

PHIL *These* walls. *This* floor. *This* ceiling. Forever.

CATH. Not forever.

PHIL. So for how long?

CATH. We don't know.

PHIL. No. Indefinitely. No fixed term. At Her Majesty's pleasure. Forever.

CATH. Phil . . .

PHIL. Look. One moment we're walking down the street, it's a nice day, anything could happen, we're thinking about this place, we're thinking about that place . . .

CATH. I thought we *weren't* thinking about that place?

PHIL. No, all right, we're not thinking about that place, not that particular place, all right, but we *could* be thinking about it, we could be thinking about whether to be thinking about it or not. Then suddenly it's all decided!

CATH. Decided?

PHIL. It would be.

CATH. Would be?

PHIL. If we decided on it.

CATH. I thought we were thinking about it?

PHIL. But that's what we're thinking about! Isn't it? We're thinking about whether to decide on it!

CATH. But, Phil, *eventually* . . .

PHIL *Eventually*. Yes. *Eventually*.

CATH. We are *going* to . . .?

PHIL. Decide? Yes. Of course. Of *course*. That's the point of thinking about things.

Pause.

Look. I'm getting at something important here, Cath. I don't know how to explain . . . Listen. Suppose we hadn't been walking down this street. Suppose we'd been walking down some other street. Yes? You can imagine that?

CATH. But we were in fact walking down this street.

PHIL. Forget that. Yes?

GATH. But . . .

PHIL. For the moment. All right? We'll come back to it. So, we're walking down another street. We see a board. Some other board. Some other house. We ring the bell – some other bell. So now we're not standing here. We're standing in some totally different room. All right?

CATH. All right.

PHIL. And what are we doing in this totally different room?

CATH. We're having precisely the same conversation.

PHIL. Exactly. We're contemplating a life looking at completely different walls. Isn't that a bit strange? Doesn't that seem slightly odd to you, Cath?

CATH. It might be somewhere worse.

PHIL. Yes! Or somewhere better.

CATH. It might be.

PHIL. But you see my point?

Pause.

CATH. Yes.

She goes to the door.

PHIL. What?

CATH. Nothing.

PHIL. Where are you going?

CATH. Away. To think about it. You said.

PHIL. Hold on.

CATH. What?

PHIL. What's going on?

CATH. What do you mean, what's going on?

PHIL. Why are you being like this all of a sudden?

CATH. Like what?

PHIL. Like this.

CATH. Come on.

She opens the door.

PHIL. Just a moment.

He closes the door.

CATH. Do you mind?

She opens the door.

PHIL. I do mind.

He closes the door.

CATH. I want to go.

She opens the door.

PHIL. I don't want to go.

He closes the door.

Not until you tell me.

CATH. Tell you what?

PHIL. What this is all about.

CATH. You know what this is all about.

PHIL. I don't know what this is all about.

CATH. Well, you do, as a matter of fact.

PHIL. Well, I don't, as a matter of fact.

Pause.

What – us?

CATH. Year after year. That's what you said. Day in, day out. Stuck here forever. No fixed term.

PHIL. I don't mean *us*!

CATH. You might find something better.

PHIL. That's what you're worrying about?

CATH *I'm* not worrying about it. *You're* worrying about it.

PHIL. Not about *us*, Cath! I'm not worrying about *us*!

CATH. That's what you're saying.

PHIL. No.

CATH. Walls, floors – us.

PHIL. Not us.

CATH. Let's go.

PHIL. Listen. Love. We're the one bit that's decided!

CATH. Are we?

PHIL. Aren't we?

CATH. I don't know.

PHIL. You don't know? You do know! You do! You know!

CATH. Yes. Well. Let's think about it.

PHIL. Let's think about it?

CATH. We're thinking about everything else.

PHIL. Exactly. Everything else. That's why we're thinking about it. Because it's everything else. We don't have to think about us. We've thought about us.

CATH. *I've* thought about us.

PHIL. *You've* thought about us. *I've* thought about us. *We've* thought about us. We're us. That's fixed. That's the problem. It's how we think about everything else. How *we* think about everything else. How we think as *us*. How we shape our world. How we decide.

CATH. How we decide?

PHIL. That's what this is all about. Isn't it?

CATH. You mean how *you* decide.

PHIL. No. How *we* decide. How you and I decide.

CATH. Oh. Well, don't worry about me. I've decided.

PHIL. You've *decided*? *You've* decided? Cath! What is all this?

CATH. One of us has to decide. One of us has to decide *something*! And if *you're* not going to decide then *I'm* going to decide, and I've decided.

PHIL. Decided what?

CATH. Decided no. So, off we go.

PHIL. Hold on.

CATH. Look, don't mess around. I've got things to do.

PHIL. Yes, but *I've* decided, too.

CATH. Well, then, that's all right.

PHIL. I've decided yes.

CATH. You've decided yes?

PHIL. Yes.

CATH. No, you haven't.

PHIL. Yes, I have.

CATH. You don't like it.

PHIL. Not much.

CATH. But you've decided yes?

PHIL. Yes.

CATH. Oh.

PHIL. Peculiar, isn't it.

CATH. Most peculiar.

PHIL. Almost as peculiar as liking it and deciding no.

CATH. I don't like it.

PHIL. Yes, you do.

CATH. I don't.

PHIL. You do.

CATH. Don't tell me what I like!

PHIL. You like it.

CATH. I hate it! As a matter of fact. So. *I* hate it. *You* hate it. *We* hate it.

PHIL. I rather like it.

CATH. What?

PHIL. I said I rather like it.

CATH. You said you *didn't* like it.

PHIL. When did I say I didn't like it?

CATH. About half-a-minute ago!

PHIL *You* said I didn't like it.

CATH. And you agreed!

PHIL. I was wrong.

CATH. What do you mean, you were wrong? How could you be wrong?

PHIL. Very easily. It's very easy to be wrong.

CATH. Not about whether you *like* something! You must know whether you *like* something or not!

PHIL. No.

CATH. I don't know what you're talking about.

PHIL. Don't you?

Pause.

CATH. You mean me.

PHIL. What?

CATH. You mean you don't like me.

PHIL. Don't like you?

CATH. Is that what you're saying?

PHIL. Just a moment. I say, I like this place. You say, You mean you don't like me . . .?

CATH. You said you *didn't* like it . . .

PHIL *You* said I didn't like it!

CATH. You said you didn't know whether you liked it or not.

PHIL. No, I didn't. What I said was . . . I don't know . . . I can't remember what I said. I don't know what we're talking about.

CATH *I* don't know what we're talking about. I don't know what's happening to us. I just want to get out of here.

Pause.

Please.

Pause.

Can we go? Please? Phil?

PHIL. Yes. I'm sorry. I just felt . . . I don't know . . .

CATH. Yes. Well. It doesn't matter.

PHIL. I just felt all kind of . . . Do you know what I mean?

CATH. Anyway . . .

PHIL. Just all kind of . . . walls and ceilings. You know?

CATH. Honestly, Phil. Sometimes . . .

PHIL. Pressing in.

CATH. I'm not trying to trap you!

PHIL. I know, I know.

CATH. I'm not trying to talk you into anything!

PHIL. It's seeing that other place. Then this place . . .

CATH. You're absolutely free to do whatever you want!

PHIL. It'll be better when we've found somewhere. When we've got everything settled.

He opens the door.

CATH. Will it?

PHIL. Won't it?

CATH. Perhaps it will.

PHIL. I think it will, Cath.

CATH. Yes . . .

She moves to go out. He stops her.

PHIL. I'm sorry, Cath. I'm sorry! My fault. All my fault. As usual.

CATH. Well, I expect *I* was . . .

PHIL. No, you weren't!

CATH. I was, as a matter of fact.

PHIL. You weren't, as a matter of fact.

CATH. Well . . .

PHIL. No. As a matter of fact. As it happens.

CATH. Anyway.

PHIL. Anyway.

He holds the door open for her. She hesitates.

CATH. Phil . . .

PHIL. What?

CATH. You do . . .?

PHIL. Do what?

CATH. Like me?

PHIL. Yes.

CATH. A bit?

PHIL. Yes.

   Pause.

   Yes! As a matter of fact. As it happens.

CATH. Just a bit?

   He closes the door.

PHIL. I love you.

CATH. Do you?

PHIL. You know I do.

CATH. Perhaps.

PHIL. I do.

CATH. Yes.

PHIL. I do.

   He kisses her.

   Yes?

CATH. Yes.

   He opens the door.

CATH. Phil . . .

PHIL. What?

   She closes the door.

   What?

CATH *I* love *you*.

PHIL. Yes.

CATH. How do you mean, yes?

PHIL. I mean I know.

CATH. You don't know, as a matter of fact.

PHIL. I do know, as a matter of fact.

CATH. Sometimes.

PHIL. Always.

CATH. Not always.

PHIL. Now, though.

CATH. Maybe.

　　They kiss.

PHIL. So . . . Yes?

CATH. Yes?

PHIL. This place.

CATH. Oh . . .!

　　She laughs.

PHIL. What?

CATH. You.

PHIL. Why?

CATH. Funny.

PHIL. Why funny?

CATH. Sweet.

　　They kiss.

PHIL. Funny if I'm sweet?

CATH. Very funny.

PHIL. I'm always sweet.

CATH. No, you're not.

PHIL. Yes, I am.

CATH. You're always arguing.

PHIL. No, I'm not.

CATH. Yes, you are.

PHIL. I'm not arguing now.

CATH. You *are* arguing now.

PHIL. Me?

CATH. You.

PHIL *I* say I'm not arguing. *You* say I'm arguing . . .

CATH. You're saying *I'm* arguing?

PHIL. All I'm saying is . . . yes.

He kisses her.

Yes. OK? Yes. Yes. Yes?

CATH. No.

PHIL. No?

CATH. Isn't that what you want me to say?

PHIL. What *I* want you to say?

CATH. Isn't it?

PHIL. I'm saying yes!

CATH. Yes, you're being very sweet.

PHIL. So?

CATH. So *I'm* being very sweet back.

PHIL. And saying no?

CATH. Then you can be very sweet back to me and say all right, no.

PHIL. Cath! Love! We're going round in circles! I'm not saying no. I'm saying yes. Quite straightforwardly – yes. All right?

Pause.

CATH. All right.

PHIL. You're agreeing?

CATH. Yes.

PHIL. So it's yes?

CATH. Yes!

Pause.

PHIL. Only you're not agreeing.

CATH. I am!

PHIL. You're not! I can see by the look on your face.

She laughs.

PHIL. What?

CATH. Nothing.

She puts her hands over her face, and laughs.

PHIL. What's funny?

CATH. Nothing's funny.

She laughs.

PHIL. So why are you laughing?

CATH. I'm not laughing.

She laughs. He waits. She stops laughing.

I'm not. In fact.

PHIL. All right . . .

CATH. All right what?

PHIL. All right, *no*.

Pause.

CATH. All right.

PHIL. That's what you're saying, isn't it? I say yes. You don't agree. You're saying no.

CATH. I'm saying no.

Enter PAT, *a woman in her sixties. She looks at each of them.*

PAT. Or do you want to think about it?

PHIL. No, no. (*To* CATH.) Well . . .

CATH. No.

PHIL. You don't just want to . . .?

CATH. No.

PHIL. No, we think . . . (*To* CATH.) Don't we?

CATH. We think it's very nice.

PHIL. Very nice!

CATH. Well, *I* think it's very nice.

PHIL. *I* think it's very nice. But I think we think that probably . . . (*To* CATH.) Well, I think *you* think . . .

CATH. *I* think?

PHIL. I thought you thought . . .?

CATH. I thought it was very nice.

PAT. You've got your bathroom, look.

PHIL. Wonderful.

PAT. You've got your kitchenette . . .

CATH. Lovely.

PAT. And your storage . . .

She draws the curtain across and back to demonstrate.

CATH. Yes!

PAT. And the roof's been done. I had the roof done. You won't have any trouble with the roof.

PHIL. Good. So we both thought that probably . . .

CATH *finds something lying behind the curtain – a battered toy dog.*

PAT. They always leave something behind when they go, don't they. There's always one thing.

PHIL. Probably it's not quite what we're looking for.

PAT. All right, love.

PHIL. I'm sorry.

PAT *leads the way to the door.*

CATH. They had a child? In here?

PAT. Little fingers, little smile. I could have eaten her!

PAT *and* PHIL *go out.* CATH *stops and takes a last look round.* PHIL *reappears.*

PHIL. What?

CATH. Nothing.

They both look round.

PHIL. You're not . . .?

CATH. No . . . No!

She puts the toy dog down and goes out. He continues to look around the room.

PHIL. No.

He goes out.

Blackout.

Scene Two

A mattress now occupies the centre of the room, with a small TV and an alarm clock on the floor beside it. A simple table, with two chairs. By the window stands a small pot plant. On the wall, a picture or two. There are a few objects carefully arranged on the shelves, including a dozen books and the toy dog. The curtain is drawn across the alcove.

PHIL and CATH are sitting on the mattress, looking at the room. She is wearing a long, shapeless jumper. He has his arms round her.

PHIL. Yes?

CATH. Yes. Yes!

PHIL. Yes . . .

   Pause.

   Or . . .

   He gets up and goes towards the shelves.

CATH. Come back!

PHIL. What?

CATH. Don't go away!

PHIL. Just . . .

CATH. What?

PHIL. This.

   He moves the toy dog to a new position.

   Better?

CATH. Better.

PHIL. Or worse?

CATH. Better. Isn't it?

PHIL. Yes. Much better.

   He returns to the mattress, and puts his arms round her.

   Yes?

CATH. Yes!

He looks round the room.

PHIL. Cath, I think . . . I *think* . . .

CATH. . . . we've got it.

PHIL. I *think.*

CATH. I think we have.

PHIL. I think we may just possibly have.

CATH *You* have.

PHIL *We* have.

CATH *You* did it.

PHIL *We* did it.

CATH. Anyway, we're there.

PHIL. We're there. No!

CATH. What?

PHIL. We're *not* there.

CATH. What's wrong?

PHIL. I'll tell you where we are, Cath.

CATH. Where?

PHIL. We're *here*!

CATH. Here?

PHIL. Here.

CATH. Here, yes.

PHIL. Not *there*.

CATH. Where?

PHIL. Anywhere!

CATH. No. Here . . .

PHIL. I'll tell you another thing, which is *when* we're here.

CATH. *When* we're here?

PHIL. Yes.

CATH. We're here *now*.

PHIL. Exactly. Not *were* here. Not *will* be here. *Are* here.

CATH *Are* here, yes.

PHIL. Now.

CATH. So . . .

PHIL. So . . .

CATH. So we can just . . . I don't know!

PHIL. Sit back.

CATH. Yes! Sit back and . . . what?

PHIL. Live. Or whatever.

CATH. Oh, love . . .

She kisses him. He looks at the shelves.

PHIL. Hold on.

CATH. What?

He jumps up and goes back to the shelves.

What are you doing?

PHIL. Nothing.

He moves the toy dog to the floor by the bed, and the alarm clock to the shelf where the dog was.

CATH. You're moving him?

PHIL. No. I just wanted to see if the clock . . .

CATH. Leave it, leave it!

She holds out her arms to him.

PHIL. Just a moment . . .

He moves it again.

CATH. You had it right before!

PHIL. Yes, but I justed wanted to try something . . .

He moves it again.

How about that?

CATH. No.

PHIL. No?

CATH. I liked him where he was before.

PHIL. What – here?

CATH. Not there . . .

PHIL. Here?

CATH. Where he was before!

PHIL. This *is* where he was before.

CATH. Anyway, it doesn't matter.

PHIL. It *does* matter!

CATH. Just leave him.

PHIL. Here?

CATH. Along a bit.

PHIL. So?

CATH. Back a bit.

PHIL. Like that?

CATH. Wonderful. Come on.

Pause.

PHIL. Only if that goes there, then this goes here . . .

He moves other items on the shelves.

And if this goes there, then *that* goes *there* . . .

Yes?

CATH. Perfect.

Pause.

PHIL. It isn't, actually.

CATH. Yes, it is.

PHIL. Not from here.

CATH. It is from here.

PHIL. Really?

CATH. Look.

She holds out her arms. He runs back to the mattress.

PHIL. Where?

CATH. Here.

She holds his head cheek to cheek with hers.

PHIL. Here?

CATH. You see?

PHIL. Yes.

CATH. Perfect.

PHIL. Only . . .

CATH. What?

PHIL. Not from there.

CATH. All right . . .

PHIL. Cath, it's *not* all right.

CATH. Yes, since we're not there.

PHIL. Not now.

CATH. We're here.

PHIL. We might be there.

CATH. But we're not.

PHIL. We *will* be there.

CATH. But we're not there now.

PHIL. No . . .

CATH. Because now we're here.

PHIL. Yes . . .

CATH. Yes?

PHIL. Yes.

They kiss.

So what are we deciding?

CATH. About what?

PHIL. About that.

CATH. We're not deciding.

PHIL. We're *not* deciding?

CATH. Not now.

PHIL. That's what we're deciding – that we're not deciding?

CATH. All right?

PHIL. So that stays like that?

CATH. For the moment.

PHIL. And not . . .

He gets up.

CATH *Now* what?

He moves the things.

PHIL. . . . like *that?*

CATH. Yes.

PHIL. Yes which?

CATH. Yes either.

PHIL. Cath!

CATH. It doesn't matter!

PHIL. Doesn't *matter?*

CATH. It's not going to start a world war if you put the dog there instead of there!

PHIL. It might! We don't know!

CATH. Don't be silly, love.

PHIL. Cath, we can't foresee what the consequences will be! We're standing at a crossroads . . .

CATH. What – putting it there or putting it there?

PHIL. Putting it there or putting it there – and there's no signpost, and we can't possibly see where the two different paths lead. All we know is that whichever one we take, that's the one we'll have taken.

CATH. We can always move it.

PHIL. That won't alter the fact that it was here to start with. It will always *have been* here. We'll have that with us forever. Forever and ever. It's like looking up at the sky at night. We're staring into infinity.

CATH. Yes, well, I don't want to think about it.

PHIL. All right, then we won't think about it.

CATH. Do you mind?

PHIL. Then on and on the effects of not thinking about it will go . . .

CATH. Yes, but let's not even talk about it.

PHIL. And if we don't even talk about it . . .

CATH. I know.

PHIL. If we don't talk about not even talking about it . . .

CATH. I know. I *know!*

PHIL. But, Cath . . .

CATH. Don't. Don't. Sorry. But just . . . don't.

Pause.

PHIL. Cath, all I'm saying is – we've got to take control.

CATH. Yes.

PHIL. Because here we are.

CATH. Here we are.

PHIL. Now.

CATH. Yes.

PHIL. As it happens.

Pause.

CATH. As it happens?

PHIL. We might not be.

CATH. What do you mean?

PHIL. We might be in some other room altogether. If we hadn't seen the board that day.

CATH. Phil, don't start all this again! We *did* see the board that day, and that's that.

PHIL But we *wouldn't* have seen the board that day if we hadn't been walking down this particular street.

CATH. But we *were* walking down this particular street.

PHIL. But *why* were we walking down this particular street?

CATH *Why* were we walking down this particular street?

PHIL. We didn't usually.

CATH. No.

PHIL. So why did we, on that particular day?

CATH. I don't know.

PHIL. No. *I* don't know!

CATH. We just did.

PHIL. We just did. Yes. We just did.

CATH. But since we *did* . . .

PHIL. Oh, sure. But isn't it a tiny bit . . .?

CATH. What?

PHIL. I don't know. A tiny bit . . . well . . .

CATH. No!

PHIL. No? I mean, look.

He gets up and walks about the room.

We wouldn't have been walking down this particular street or any other particular street if . . . well . . . if we'd never met.

CATH. Never met? What are you talking about? What is all this? We did meet, we did meet!

PHIL. Yes, but we shouldn't have met if I hadn't gone to that place where you were that day.

CATH. No . . .

PHIL. And I shouldn't have gone to that place if I hadn't known that man.

CATH. All right.

PHIL. And I shouldn't have known that man if I hadn't walked up that mountain, and I shouldn't have walked up that mountain if there hadn't been a mountain to walk up, and there wouldn't have been a mountain to walk up if the rock strata hadn't been tilted the way they are, and the rock strata wouldn't have been tilted the way they are if the earth had cooled down differently five thousand million years ago, and if it had, Cath, if it had, if the earth had cooled down slightly differently five thousand million years ago, then I wouldn't be here now – *you* wouldn't be here now – you'd be sitting in some completely different room with some completely different man.

CATH. No, I shouldn't.

PHIL. Yes, you would. If you'd met someone else instead of me.

CATH. If I'd met someone else instead of you?

PHIL. Yes.

CATH. I shouldn't have fallen in love with them!

PHIL. Yes, you would. Of course you would. If I hadn't been there. You'd have fallen in love with *someone*.

CATH. You mean, *you* would?

PHIL. All right.

CATH *You'd* be sitting here with some completely different woman?

PHIL. Yes! No . . .

He goes back to the mattress and puts his arms round her.

CATH. You would, wouldn't you.

PHIL. No. As it happens.

CATH. Yes, you would. I know you would.

Pause.

PHIL. I'll put it back.

He gets up and moves everything back to its orginal position.

This was here. Yes? This was here . . . All right?

CATH. No.

PHIL. Cath! I've put it *back!*

CATH. I don't know what you mean, it all just *happened*.

PHIL. I mean things happened that we didn't decide . . .

CATH. But we *did* decide!

PHIL. In the end.

CATH. We decided about *this* place!

PHIL. Exactly. We took over . . .

CATH. We walked down the street, we saw the board, we looked at this place, and we *decided!*

PHIL. Yes, so now we've got to go *on* deciding.

CATH. 'It all just happened'! It *didn't* all just happen! We made it happen!

PHIL. That's what I'm saying! We're saying the same thing!

CATH. This is us.

PHIL. Yes! So now we have to go on deciding together till death us do part.

CATH. We *have* gone on deciding. I don't know what you're talking about. We put this here, we put that there.

She jumps up and moves things round.

We could have put this there and that here.

PHIL. We could have done.

He moves them back.

But we didn't.

CATH. But we still could.

She moves them back again.

PHIL. What are you doing?

CATH. We could put anything anywhere!

PHIL. Cath! We had it almost right!

CATH. We don't have to have things right! We can have them wrong if we want to!

PHIL. Yes, but we don't *want* them wrong!

CATH *I* want them wrong!

She moves the mattress.

PHIL. Cath – not the *bed!*

CATH. I *want* the bed here!

PHIL. You can't *want* it here if it's *wrong!*

CATH *I* can! I do!

PHIL. Cath, stop! Stop. Stop. Stop.

CATH. You're always telling me what I want.

PHIL. OK, you want the bed here. May I ask one simple question?

CATH *Why* do I want the bed here?

PHIL. No. How do you *know* you want it here?

CATH. How do I *know* I want it here? Don't be silly.

PHIL. I'm not being silly. How, in actual fact, do you *know* you want it here?

CATH. I just do.

PHIL. Oh. You just do.

CATH. All right?

PHIL. All right. Fine. Wonderful.

CATH. So then the television goes here . . .

PHIL. Hold on. You just know you want it here. I just know you *don't* want it here.

CATH. You just know I don't want it here?

PHIL. Yes.

CATH. So how do you just know that?

PHIL. I just do. The same as you just do.

CATH. But I'm me and you're you!

PHIL. Also because I know you're simply trying to make a point. Because no one in the entire world could possibly want the bed here.

CATH. Except me.

PHIL. Anyway, I *don't* want it here.

CATH. That's another matter.

PHIL. Cath, come on! What I mean is, we have to agree!

CATH. No, we don't.

PHIL. So how do we decide?

CATH. We can fight.

PHIL. Fight?

CATH. Why not?

PHIL. How?

CATH. Like this.

She grabs his ankle and tips him backwards on to the mattress.

I've won!

PHIL. That's not fair!

CATH. So the bed goes here.

PHIL. But I wasn't ready!

He jumps up.

All right. If you want to fight, we'll fight.

They stand on the mattress, facing each other.

All right?

CATH. All right.

PHIL. You say, then.

CATH. What do you want me to say?

PHIL. Say ready steady.

CATH. Ready steady?

PHIL. Yes . . .

CATH. Go!

She grabs his ankle, and tips him over backwards.

PHIL. Don't be ridiculous!

CATH. What?

He gets up.

PHIL. You can't just say go!

CATH. I said ready steady!

PHIL. You said ready steady query.

CATH. I didn't say ready steady query.

PHIL. You did!

CATH. I said ready steady go!

She grabs his ankle, and tips him over backwards.

PHIL. Cath, that's *cheating*!

He attempts to get up. She squats on top of him.

Get off! Cath, will you get off me . . .? I shall get angry in a minute . . . You're crushing things . . . Agh! Pax! Cath, I said pax . . .

She pulls the duvet up around them.

CATH. We've fallen into a snowdrift! We're at the South Pole!

PHIL. Cath, stop messing around . . .

CATH. The wind's howling. It's dark. We don't know where we are.

She lies full length on top of him, in the confusion of the duvet.

PHIL. What's all this?

CATH. We'll freeze to death. We'll die. The wind's blowing us away . . .

They begin to roll away off the mattress, wrapped in the duvet. There is a knocking at the door.

We're out of control!

PHIL. What's that banging?

CATH. Stop us, someone! We're going to roll off the edge of the world . . .!

PHIL. Hold on . . .

CATH. Help! Help!

More knocking at the door.

PHIL. Cath . . .

PAT (*off*). Cath?

They stop rolling.

Are you all right?

They sit up.

Cath!

PHIL *begins to get to his feet.* CATH *restrains him.*

CATH (*whispers*). She'll go away . . .

They wait.

PAT (*off*). Cath, it's me.

More urgent knocking.

PHIL (*to* PAT). Coming!

He goes to open the door.

CATH (*whispers*). Wait!

PHIL (*whispers*). What?

She indicates the state of the room.

PHIL (*whispers*). We can't start . . .

PAT (*off*). Phil?

PHIL (*to* PAT). Yes, coming!

CATH (*whispers*). Bed!

She pulls the mattress back.

Where?

PHIL (*whispers*). Anywhere!

CATH (*whispers*). Here?

PHIL (*whispers*). Yes! No!

CATH (*whispers*). Just tell me!

PHIL (*whispers*). Here.

CATH (*whispers*). Yes?

PHIL (*whispers*). Yes.

He goes to open the door.

CATH (*whispers*). Wait!

She hurriedly puts all the other things back in their original positions. The door is shaken in its frame.

PAT (*off*). Phil? What's happening?

PHIL. Coming! Coming! (*Whispers.*) Yes?

CATH (*whispers*). Yes! Yes!

PHIL *opens the door.*

PHIL. Come in.

PAT. Where's Cath?

CATH. Come in!

PAT. Oh, there you are. As long as you're all right . . . I won't come in.

She comes in.

I'm not coming in.

CATH. Sit down.

PHIL. Sit down.

She remains standing.

PAT. I don't want to keep running up the stairs.

CATH. No, please.

PAT. Dropping in all the time.

CATH. Sit down!

She remains standing.

PAT. Only – crash on the ceiling.

PHIL. Oh, sorry, yes, that was me. I fell over.

PAT. Then crash again.

PHIL. Yes, I got up, and . . .

CATH. We were talking about where things should go.

PAT. Then crash a third time.

PHIL. We were messing around.

PAT. I thought – oh no, here we go again. Last couple up here – just like you – not a stick of furniture – nothing – all over each other. Honey this, lovey that. All very nice, only then of course the shouting started, then the screaming started. 'You swore on your mother's grave!' That's her. Scream scream. That's *him*! Screaming his lungs out! I've never heard anything like it! This door? I thought they'd have it off the hinges. Slam! She goes running down the stairs. Meanwhile everything up here's going smash. Smash smash smash. All the glasses, all the plates. Then they had the *baby*.

Pause.

So I hear crash on the ceiling tonight I think, here we go again.

CATH. Yes. Thank you.

PHIL. Sit down.

She remains standing.

PAT. I shouldn't have told you all that. You want to come into an empty room. Fresh paint, a few bits and pieces of your own, blank page, chapter one, nothing ever happened in the world before.

PHIL. Anyway.

CATH. Sit down.

She remains standing.

PAT. You could put the table here, look. Then the mattress could go there.

CATH. Yes!

PHIL. Yes!

PAT. Peter's bed was there. David's bed was there. This was Peter and David's room. Lucy was downstairs opposite me.

CATH. Yes, I'm sorry . . .

PAT. Go through all that again? No, thank you! Up and down the stairs. Bad dreams, drinks of water. 'Now if you two don't tidy this room I don't know what I shall do!' Slaps, fights. Hugs, kisses. 'This room – it's a disgrace!' Crash crash crash on the ceiling – what are they up to up there? Then nothing – silence – they're out all night – where are they? You two come wandering in, stars in your eyes, you think a bed to sleep in, a table to eat at, that's all you need – you don't know what you're starting. Now what? David's up North, Peter's all over the place, he's very big in Europe, Lucy's living with some woman in a caravan – 'Mum, I'm a lesbian.' Meanwhile I've got their old vaccination records downstairs, I've got microscopes, I've got electrical this, I've got electrical that, I've got a whole cat-basket full of doll's clothes, I can't move down there. While here you are, mattress on the floor, one rickety table, you think it's not going to happen to you. You think, poor old soul, comes running up here at the slightest squeak, she feels sorry for herself. I'll tell you who the poor old soul feels sorry for – she feels sorry for you.

CATH. Yes. Well . . .

PHIL. Yes.

PAT *sits down on one of the chairs.*

PAT. Then we put Mum in here. Bed there, her piano there, her old walnut dining-room suite. All her knick-knacks. It was like a furniture shop. You couldn't move! I said, 'Mum, this is worse than the boys!' She said, 'You won't have to put up with it for very long, Pat.' Oh, won't I? I put up with it for seven years. Bang bang on the ceiling. Up and down the stairs. 'Never mind, Pat, you won't have to put up with it for much longer now.' She died in my arms! Gave me a smile and died in my arms!

She weeps. CATH *sits down on the other chair.* PHIL *remains standing.*

CATH. I'm sorry . . .

PAT *I'm* not. I'm glad. Glad you can get it all behind you. Settle down. Be on your own. Not have to think about other people all day long. You? You've got it all to come. You think I envy you? I don't. I don't.

CATH. No.

PHIL. No.

PAT. I made up a bed in here for Eric. This was the year after I lost Mum. He'd come up here nights when his cough was bad and then he could cough away on his own. Cough cough. Cough cough. All night, no rest from it. Cough cough. Cough cough. He thought I couldn't hear him up here. I could hear him. Cough cough. But of course I never said, so he thought I was asleep, it was easier for *him.* Poor lamb. Coughed his heart out. He coughed *my* heart out. Him awake up here, me awake down there. Poor old love.

CATH. When did he . . .?

PAT. Four years ago. They took his lung out, but it was all over him by then, he was riddled with it. Seven weeks in the hospital, nine weeks in the nursing home, and that was it. That was the end of the story. So it's all behind me. And if you think I'd want to be you, one mattress, one table, honey this, lovey that, and everything still to come, then you're much mistaken. So what have you got to say to that?

CATH. Oh . . .

PHIL. Well . . .

PAT. Nothing. Right.

PAT *goes out. Pause.*

CATH. Poor Pat.

PHIL. Not what she said.

CATH. No. Poor love.

PHIL. So Arthur was here. Cyril was there.

CATH. Don't.

PHIL. Don't what?

CATH. It's sad.

PHIL. Heartbreaking . . . Cough cough.

CATH. Phil!

PHIL. She can't hear.

CATH. I don't care.

PHIL. Cough cough.

CATH. Anyway, she might.

PHIL. Cough cough?

CATH. She heard you before.

PHIL. That was crash crash.

CATH. She heard *him*.

PHIL. That was *cough cough*.

CATH. Sh!

PHIL *I* went cough cough.

CATH. But if she was *there* . . .

She nods at the door.

PHIL. Where?

She nods at the door again.

Outside the door?

CATH. Sh!

PHIL. She isn't.

CATH. She could be.

PHIL. She wouldn't.

CATH. Why not? It's her landing.

PHIL. It's our door.

CATH. It's her house.

Pause. Then PHIL *goes to the door.*

CATH. What?

PHIL. Open it.

CATH. Don't!

PHIL. See if she's there.

CATH. No!

PHIL. Why not?

CATH. Because supposing she was.

PHIL. What do you mean?

CATH. We open the door . . .

PHIL. Yes?

CATH. And there she is.

PHIL. So there she is.

CATH. Then what?

PHIL. I don't know. We say . . .

CATH. What do we say?

PHIL. 'Hello.'

CATH. Don't be silly.

PHIL. 'Oh, there you are.'

CATH. No.

PHIL. No?

CATH. No . . . Or perhaps we should.

PHIL. All right.

CATH. Go on.

PHIL. Open it?

CATH. Open it!

PHIL *puts his ear to the door.*

PHIL *(whispers).* I can hear her!

CATH *(whispers).* You can't.

PHIL *(whispers).* I can!

He suddenly opens the door. PAT *is standing on the threshold. He automatically closes the door on her again in surprise, looks at* CATH, *then immediately reopens it.*

PHIL. Sorry.

CATH. Sorry.

PHIL. I'd no idea . . .

PAT. Here. Eric's favourite.

She brings in a chair.

Don't worry. I'm not going to keep running upstairs. Last thing
you want is people messing you around, bringing you their old
junk.

CATH. Oh, Pat . . .!

PAT. Oh, Pat what?

CATH. We couldn't.

PAT. Couldn't you?

CATH (*to* PHIL). Could we?

PAT. I don't want it. I hate the sight of it.

PHIL. Yes, but . . .

PAT. What – does Eric mind? I don't know, my loves. That's the
wonderful thing. I didn't have to ask him.

PAT goes out. PHIL *closes the door.*

CATH. Was she out there all the time?

PHIL. I don't know. This chair . . .

CATH. Do you think she heard?

PHIL. Cath, we can't have things imposed upon us. We can't have
things we didn't choose ourselves.

CATH. We never thanked her.

PHIL. No. So. Decision . . .

*He takes the chair to the alcove. He pulls back the curtain. A world of
hanging clothes, cardboard boxes, cleaning materials, and odd
random possessions is revealed for an instant. He puts the chair in
with it, and pulls the curtain across.*

Yes?

CATH. In there?

PHIL. In the junk.

CATH. Not just in there.

PHIL. Not junk?

CATH. My old things.

PHIL *Your* old things. *My* old things. Junk.

CATH. Yes. Well.

PHIL. So – in here?

CATH. All right.

PHIL. Unanimous?

CATH. Yes . . . Only . . .

PHIL. What?

CATH. If she comes back?

PHIL. She won't come back.

CATH. She will come back!

PHIL. I say she won't. *We* say she won't. Yes?

CATH. But we can't just . . .

PHIL. We can just. We will just.

CATH. Phil, be realistic.

PHIL. Our piece of space. Yes? Our bit of world. We say.

CATH. Of course. Only if she comes to the door . . .

PHIL. So no Pat. No Eric. No Eric's chair or Eric's old
underpants. No Lucy, no David, no Peter. No old mother. No
coughs, no screams. No muddle. No mess. No *junk*.

CATH. All right. Only . . .

PHIL. Decision. Yes?

CATH. Yes. Only . . .

A knock at the door. Pause. Another knock.

PAT. Oh, Cath . . .

Pause. CATH *and* PHIL *look at each other.*

Cath?

CATH *goes to the door.*

PHIL. Wait.

He gets the chair out from behind the curtain, and puts it in the middle of the room. CATH *opens the door.*

PAT. Oh, still there? I thought it'd be behind that curtain by now.

CATH. Oh . . .

PHIL. No . . .

CATH. No!

PAT. No, Cath, just to say if you don't want it – put it out for the dustman.

CATH. Of course we want it . . .

But PAT *has already gone.*

PHIL. So, dustman?

CATH. No.

PHIL. Junk?

CATH. Yes.

He puts the chair back behind the curtain.

CATH. But you don't mean no *children*. Do you? We'd like *children*.

PHIL *turns in surprise.*

PHIL. Children?

Cases and boxes dislodged by the chair come tumbling out into the room.

CATH. Wouldn't we?

Blackout.

Scene Three

The mattress has been moved to a less dominant position, and the table and two chairs have taken its place. The pot plant has noticeably grown. There is no sign of the third chair.

CATH *is wearing the same loose jumper as before.* PHIL *is wearing an identical one. They are sitting on opposite sides of the table, working on books and papers.*

PHIL *stops working and watches* CATH, *irritated.*

PHIL. What?

Silence. CATH *works.*

I said 'what?'

CATH. What do you mean, 'what?'?

PHIL. What do you mean, what do I mean? I mean 'what?'

CATH. I didn't say anything.

PHIL. No.

CATH. What?

PHIL. I rather thought not.

CATH. What is all this?

PHIL. What is all what?

CATH. What are you talking about?

PHIL. Nothing.

CATH. Nothing. Oh. That's interesting.

PHIL. Yes. Because that's what you said.

CATH. What's what I said?

PHIL. Nothing.

CATH. Oh.

PHIL. *You* said nothing. *I* said nothing. Nothing was said. That's what I was remarking upon.

Pause.

CATH. So why are you looking like that?

PHIL. Why am I looking like *what*?

CATH. That.

PHIL. This?

CATH. Yes.

PHIL. I'm looking like this because this is what I look like.

CATH. No, it isn't.

PHIL. Yes, it is.

CATH. You know perfectly well how you're looking.

PHIL. I *don't* know how I'm looking. As a matter of fact. Human eyes being located where they are located. I know how *you're* looking. *You* don't know how you're looking. *You* know how *I'm* looking. *I* don't, though. All I know, since it's not a matter of observation but a matter of logic, is that whatever I'm looking like, I'm looking like it because it's what I look like.

Pause.

Also because of your saying 'what?' like that.

CATH. What?

PHIL. Exactly.

CATH. I don't know what you're talking about. *I* said 'what?'? *You* said 'what?'

PHIL. We both said 'what?'

CATH. So?

PHIL. I didn't say it like that.

CATH. Like what?

PHIL. Inauthentically.

CATH. What?

PHIL. You see?

CATH. Just a moment. I said 'what' *inauthentically*?

PHIL. Right.

CATH. How can anyone say 'what' *inauthentically*?

PHIL. Very easily. By saying 'what?' when they don't mean 'what?' By saying 'what?' when they know the answer to the question perfectly well.

CATH. The answer to what question?

PHIL. You know what question.

CATH. I *don't* know what question. I've no idea what you're talking about.

Pause.

PHIL. Look, let's go right back to the beginning. Let's try to reconstruct this conversation before we've forgotten how it went. You said 'what?' . . .

CATH *You* said 'what?' You said it first. I wasn't saying anything.

PHIL. All right. *I* said 'what?' That's true. I said 'what?', then you said 'what?' That's right. That's the point I'm making. Because you knew perfectly well why I'd said 'what?' I said 'what?' because you hadn't said anything. You knew that. So that when you said 'what?' . . .

CATH (*holds up her hand*). Phil. Stop. All right. This is about what it was about last time, is it?

PHIL. No? Why? What was it about last time?

CATH. Who's playing games now?

Pause.

PHIL. Oh, no!

CATH. You knew.

PHIL. I didn't know.

CATH. I told you yesterday.

PHIL. You said she *might* be coming up.

CATH. Thank you.

PHIL. You mean she *is* coming up?

CATH. I mean she *might* be coming up.

PHIL. Might be coming up when?

CATH. I don't know.

PHIL. Any time?

CATH. She didn't say.

Pause.

PHIL. I thought we'd agreed.

CATH. Agreed?

PHIL. Agreed not to ask her without agreeing first.

CATH. I didn't ask her.

PHIL. Oh. She just said she was coming?

CATH. She said she might be coming.

PHIL. Any time?

CATH. Some time.

PHIL. So *you* said . . .?

CATH. Phil, she's on her own down there!

PHIL. And we're having such fun up here.

Pause. She works.

So, when you agreed not to ask her without agreeing first, you didn't mean it. Your agreement was *inauthentic*.

Pause. He works. She watches him. Then she gets up and drags the mattress back to where it was in the previous scene.

PHIL. What's happening?

CATH. That's what this is all about.

PHIL. That?

CATH. Isn't it?

PHIL. No!

CATH. Really?

PHIL. I agreed!

CATH. You agreed, yes. But your agreement was . . .

PHIL. What?

CATH. You tell me.

PHIL. Inauthentic? Is that what you're saying? My agreement was *inauthentic*?

She sits down and resumes her work. Pause.

Look. Look. I wanted it here. Yes. That's true. You wanted it there. I was making a simple point, and you didn't accept it, but I'll make it again. The things around us, it seems to me, should give natural expression to the form of our life. Now, what is the centre of our life? The centre of our life is our being together. Yes? Our being one. Yes? What is the physical embodiment of our being one? Our making love. Where do we make love?

CATH. On this chair, sometimes.

PHIL. Sometimes.

CATH. On that chair.

PHIL. Never mind the chairs. We make love on this bed. If making love is at the centre of our life, then this bed ought to be in the centre of the room. That's all I'm saying. I felt that this arrangement was more . . .

CATH. Authentic.

PHIL. Authentic, yes. But you didn't accept this. You argued – I hope I've got this right – that there is some natural order in the universe according to which the table and chairs should be more central than the bed.

CATH. I just said there was something a bit funny about having the bed in the middle of the room.

PHIL. A bit funny, yes.

He drags the mattress back to the periphery.

We certainly don't want anything in this room that's a bit funny.

CATH *gets up.*

What?

She drags the mattress into the centre.

CATH. If we're talking about the natural order of things in the universe then the natural order of things in the universe is where you want them, so we might as well just put them there and have done with it.

PHIL. No!

He drags it back to the periphery.

If you don't agree then putting it there is completely . . .

CATH. Where did you pick up this ridiculous word?

PHIL. What word?

CATH. Inauthentic.

PHIL. I didn't say inauthentic.

CATH. No, you were just about to.

PHIL. I wasn't, as a matter of fact.

CATH. Oh, what were you going to say?

PHIL. I'm not going to tell you.

Pause. She laughs.

CATH. Phil, honestly!

Pause. He laughs.

Honestly!

Pause. They have stopped laughing.

PHIL. Also, you're wearing my jumper again.

CATH. This? This is *my* jumper.

He smells the arm of the jumper he is wearing.

PHIL *This* is your jumper.

She sniffs the arm of the jumper she is wearing.

CATH. It's not!

PHIL. It is, as a matter of fact.

CATH. Anyway, since they're exactly the same . . .

PHIL. They're not exactly the same!

CATH. What's the difference?

PHIL. What's the difference? One's yours and one's mine. That's
the difference.

CATH. Phil, you're such a prick.

Pause.

PHIL. Come here.

CATH. What?

PHIL. Come here!

He puts his arms round her.

CATH. What are you doing?

PHIL. What do you mean, what am I doing? I'm putting my arms round you.

CATH. You're smelling my jumper.

PHIL. I'm not smelling your jumper. I'm not even smelling *my* jumper. I've got my nose closed. What I'm doing is . . .

He draws her down so that they are kneeling.

. . . taking my jumper off.

He slowly begins to pull up the jumper she is wearing.

CATH. What, now?

PHIL. Now.

CATH. Here?

PHIL. The centre of the room.

CATH. So?

PHIL. The centre of the world.

CATH. But the bed's *there*.

PHIL. Exactly!

There is a tap on the door.

PAT (*off*). Cath?

Pause. She pulls the jumper down again.

CATH. Phil, I had to!

Pause.

PHIL. Yes . . .

He gets up and goes to the door.

CATH. Wait!

PHIL. What?

She gets PAT's chair out from behind the curtain and sets it at the table.

PHIL *opens the door*.

PAT. Wrong moment?

PHIL. No, no.

CATH. Come in.

PAT *enters*.

PAT. I'm not staying.

PHIL. Sit down.

PAT. You don't want me up here at all hours.

PHIL. Any time. (*To* CATH.) Yes?

CATH. Sit down.

PHIL. Stop us arguing.

PAT. Oh, I can guess what that was about. 'What? Not *her* again?'

PHIL. Your chair, Madam.

PAT. Runs out from behind that curtain every time it hears me coming.

PHIL. Sits here waiting for you. Pining away. Its little paws in the air.

PAT. Not my chair.

PHIL. Eric's chair.

PAT. He always sat in that chair.

PAT *sits down on one of the other chairs*. PHIL *offers Eric's chair to* CATH.

PHIL. Eric's chair . . .

CATH *sits down on the other original chair*.

CATH (*to* PAT). Tea? Coffee? Anything?

PAT. No thanks, love. No, anybody else sat there he wouldn't say anything.

PHIL *sits down in Eric's chair.*

PHIL. But you'd know.

PAT. 'What's the matter?' I'd go to him.

PHIL. 'Nothing,' he'd go.

CATH *looks at him.*

What?

She looks away.

PAT. 'Oh, your chair.' 'It doesn't matter.'

PHIL. You'd have to tell them.

PAT. I'd have to tell them. 'You're sitting in Eric's chair!'

PHIL. Then afterwards . . .

PAT. Afterwards, oh! 'You shouldn't have said that!' 'Said what?' 'Said it was my chair!'

PHIL. Always your fault, isn't it.

CATH *looks at him.*

What?

CATH. Nothing.

PAT. What?

PHIL. Nothing.

Pause.

PAT. Oh, that's much better, Cath. Your mattress. Up in the corner there.

CATH. Oh. Yes.

PHIL. You like it?

PAT. Looked a bit funny out here in the middle of the room.

PHIL. A bit funny?

PAT. I never liked to say.

PHIL *(to* CATH). A bit funny. You see?

PAT. Oh, now I've done it.

PHIL. No, you tell her, Pat. She won't listen to me.

PAT. Only the last lot were like that. Bedclothes everywhere. You didn't know where to look. Then of course it all started. Crash. Bang. I came running up here. Nothing but broken glass and blood all over his face. Carry-cot standing in the middle of it all. Poor little mite.

PHIL *(to* CATH). Now he's in prison, she's in a better world.

PAT. For all I know.

CATH. Phil doesn't want it up there.

PAT. Oh, he's the one?

PHIL *I* don't want it up there? I *put* it up there!

CATH. He thinks it's inauthentic.

PAT. Oh, I see. It's what?

CATH. Inauthentic.

PHIL. Inauthentic? Is that what I think?

CATH. It's his new word.

PHIL *(to* PAT). I say these strange things.

CATH. The last one was 'over-determinate'.

PHIL *(to* PAT). 'Over-determinate'! Can you imagine?

CATH. Over-determinate is what it would be if we had more than two chairs.

PHIL. More than three chairs, I think you mean, my love.

CATH. More than three chairs.

PHIL *(to* PAT). We agree about some things.

CATH. Also *indeterminate*.

PHIL. We don't agree about indeterminate.

CATH. Indeterminate is what it is if the bathroom door isn't closed.

PHIL *(to* CATH*).* Not at all. It doesn't have to be closed.

CATH. What do you mean? It has to be closed!

PHIL. No, it can be open.

CATH. It can't be open!

PHIL. It can be *fully* open.

CATH. Oh, *fully* open . . .

PHIL. But not half-open.

CATH *(to* PAT*).* Not half-open.

PHIL. Which is what it is now.

CATH *(to* PAT*).* Here we go again!

PHIL *(to* PAT*).* Yes, because she's always half-doing things! If she puts a book down it's half on the table and half off the table. If she's doing the washing up she half does it and half doesn't. If it's her turn to clean the room she cleans half of it and then she stops!

CATH Don't drag Pat into all this nonsense!

PHIL. Don't drag Pat into it? You're telling *me* not to drag Pat into it? Pat – did *I* drag you into this?

PAT. I'm not saying a word, my loves.

PHIL *(to* CATH*).* You see?

CATH. See what?

PAT. Leave me right out of it, my doves.

CATH. I know what Pat thinks.

PHIL. Oh, you know what Pat thinks?

PAT. None of us says anything we can't say anything wrong.

CATH. Yes.

PHIL. Yes!

PAT. So, thank you, Cath, thank you, Phil . . .

She gets to her feet.

PHIL. Where are you going?

CATH. Don't be silly.

PHIL. We're not going to have a *row*. Are we, my love?

CATH *I'm* not going to have a row.

PHIL *I'm* not going to have a row.

CATH. Sit down!

PAT sits, reluctantly.

PAT. Only I don't want to start anything.

CATH. You're not.

PHIL. You're stopping it.

PAT. Yes. Well.

Pause.

That plant's coming on, Cath.

CATH. Yes.

PHIL. Yes!

CATH. What?

PHIL. Nothing.

PAT. It likes being by the window there.

PHIL. It does indeed.

Pause.

PAT. Have I said something?

CATH. No.

PHIL. No, no. No, no.

CATH (*to* PHIL). What?

PHIL. Nothing.

Pause.

PAT. Eric was a great one for pot-plants. 'You know what you are?' I used to say to him. 'You're pot-potty.'

Pause.

CATH (*to* PHIL). I don't know what you're talking about!

PHIL (*to* PAT). *It* likes it there. *She* wants it *here*.

CATH. I *don't* want it here!

PHIL. Oh. I thought you did?

CATH *You* want it here!

PHIL *I* want it here?

CATH. You said 'It has to go here'!

PHIL. Yes. If the bed stays *there*.

CATH. Pat . . .

PHIL. Never mind Pat. Pat can see for herself. If the bed stays *there* then there's a space *here* . . .

He gets up to demonstrate.

CATH (*to* PAT). There's a space, you see.

PHIL. . . . so that if you want the bed *there* then you want the plant *here*.

CATH. I *don't* want the plant here!

PHIL. Then you *should* want the plant here.

CATH. I *should* want the plant here?

PHIL. Logically.

CATH. Oh, don't start saying 'logically'!

PHIL. No, but it's half-doing things again.

CATH. Phil, I shall murder you.

PHIL. No, you won't. You'll half-murder me.

PAT. Listen, my loves . . .

CATH. Yes, tell him, will you, Pat?

PHIL. All right, let's ask Pat.

PAT. You *can't* put the plant there, because there's no light.

CATH. That's precisely what I'm saying.

PHIL. That's precisely the point I'm making.

PAT. So put the *chair* there.

She moves Eric's chair into the empty space.

PHIL. The chair?

CATH. We don't want the chair there, do we?

PAT. You don't want the chair there?

CATH (*to* PHIL). *You* don't want the chair there?

PHIL *I* don't want the chair there!

CATH. I don't want the chair there.

PAT. Right, put the chair *here*. Put the TV there . . .

PHIL. We can't have the TV there.

CATH. We can't have the chair there.

PAT. Right. TV here. Chair here. Clock here. Then move the table *here* . . .

PHIL. No, no, no, no!

CATH. Not the table!

PAT. Or *here*, look . . .

CATH. No!

PHIL. No!

PAT. TV here . . .

PHIL. It doesn't work there!

PAT. Chair here . . .

CATH. No, stop, wait . . .

PAT. Then slide your mattress over *here* . . .

CATH *Pat*!

PAT. What?

CATH. Just . . . leave it, will you?

PAT. Leave what?

PHIL. Leave everything.

PAT. Leave it where?

PHIL. Where it is.

PAT. Where it is?

PHIL. Perfect.

CATH. Thank you.

Pause. The room is in chaos.

PAT. I was only trying to settle the argument.

CATH. Yes. Thank you.

PHIL. You've settled it.

CATH. Thank you.

PHIL. You see?

He puts his arm round CATH. *Pause.*

PAT. I'll put it back.

PHIL. No!

CATH. No!

PAT. You don't want it like *this*!

PHIL. We want it like *this*.

CATH. Thank you.

PHIL. Thank you.

   Pause.

PAT. You don't want that chair, either.

   She picks up Eric's chair and takes it to the door with her.

CATH. Yes, we do.

PHIL. Of course we do.

PAT. That was Eric's chair.

PHIL. We know.

PAT. I'll give it to the jumble.

CATH. We *want* it!

PHIL. We love it!

   He takes it from her.

PAT. You don't want me coming up you've only got to say.

CATH. No!

PHIL. Yes!

CATH. Pat!

   PAT *goes out. Pause.*

PHIL. Sob sob.

CATH. I'll go.

PHIL *I'll* go.

CATH. You get this place straight.

PHIL. Yes . . .

They look at it.

I can't remember exactly where the table was.

CATH. Here.

They put the table back where it was at the beginning of the scene.

PHIL. Yes. Yes.

He replaces the two chairs and the TV.

Yes?

CATH. Yes.

She goes to the door.

PHIL. Cath!

CATH. What?

He replaces the mattress where it was at the beginning of the scene.

PHIL. I like it.

CATH. You don't.

PHIL. I do.

CATH. We'll talk about it.

She goes to the door.

PHIL. Cath!

CATH. What?

PHIL. I like *you.*

CATH. You don't.

PHIL. I do.

Pause.

CATH. Do you?

He kisses her.

A bit?

PHIL. A bit.

He kisses her.

Do you like me?

CATH. No.

PHIL. Yes, you do.

CATH. No, I don't.

He kisses her.

I dreamt last night you were hanging me up and putting me away.

PHIL. Oh. Was that nice?

CATH. No.

PHIL. I'm always behaving badly in your dreams.

CATH. Yes.

PHIL. I'm sorry.

CATH. No, you're not. You think it's my fault.

PHIL *Your* fault?

CATH. You think I'm dreaming aggressively.

PHIL. No, I don't. I think you dream very nicely.

CATH. You were putting me behind that curtain.

PHIL. I must have got carried away.

CATH. You never dream of me.

PHIL. Yes, I do.

CATH. When?

PHIL. Often.

CATH. What am I doing?

PHIL. Nice things.

CATH. Such as?

PHIL. I can't remember.

CATH. No.

PHIL. Hanging me up and putting me away.

CATH. You wouldn't like it if I did.

PHIL. I should, as a matter of fact.

CATH. Not if I did it the way you did it to me.

PHIL. That was terrible.

CATH. You're a nasty old man.

He kisses her.

Always making rows.

PHIL. We don't have rows.

CATH. We do have rows.

PHIL. No, we don't.

CATH. Yes, we do.

PHIL. I hate having rows.

CATH. You love having rows.

PHIL. I quite like having rows.

CATH. You're a nasty, pedantic, narrow-minded, quarrelsome, bullying old man.

PHIL. Yes.

CATH. Yes!

PHIL *You* quite like having rows.

CATH. No, I don't.

PHIL. Yes, you do.

He kisses her.

You do.

He kisses her.

Anyway, we don't really have rows, do we?

CATH. Don't we?

PHIL. What do we have rows about?

CATH. Everything.

PHIL. Everything?

CATH. The bed.

PHIL. Oh, well, the bed.

CATH. The table. The chairs.

PHIL. Not *this* chair.

CATH. No?

PHIL. No. Back behind the curtain.

CATH. Poor Pat.

PHIL. Sob sob.

CATH. All on her own down there.

She goes towards the door.

PHIL. Cath!

He runs up behind her.

CATH. What?

He pulls up the jumper he is wearing, and pulls it down over her head, so that she is inside it with him, her arms trapped, her head emerging from the top beside his.

PHIL. Closer together. Yes?

CATH. All right.

PHIL. No more rows.

CATH. No?

PHIL. We can't have rows inside the same jumper.

CATH. Can't we?

PHIL. Not if we're doing everything together. Come on . . .

He pushes one of her feet forward with his.

CATH. What are you doing?

PHIL. Whatever *you're* doing.

They begin to move about the room as one.

CATH. Where are we going?

PHIL. Wherever we're going.

CATH. Phil!

PHIL. One flesh. One heart . . .

CATH. We'll fall over!

PHIL. One pair of legs.

CATH. One pair of heads.

PHIL. But side by side. Seeing everything from each other's point of view.

CATH. Thinking downstairs we go.

They head towards the door.

PHIL. Thinking upstairs we stay.

They head away from the door.

CATH. And upstairs we stay.

PHIL. One pair of hands.

They pick up Eric's chair.

CATH. Not picking up the chair.

PHIL. Picking up the chair.

CATH. And putting it here.

They move it towards the table.

PHIL. And putting it *here*.

They put it behind the curtain.

CATH. And putting it there.

PHIL. You see how easy it is?

CATH. What?

PHIL. Deciding where everything goes.

CATH. We didn't decide.

PHIL. We must have decided.

CATH. Why?

PHIL. If we did it.

CATH. We just did it.

PHIL. Right, we'll watch out.

CATH. Watch out for what?

PHIL. To catch ourselves deciding. All right?

CATH. All right.

PHIL. All right . . . *now.*

CATH. What's happening?

PHIL. We're deciding.

CATH. Are we?

PHIL. Aren't we?

CATH. Deciding what?

PHIL. What to do next.

Pause.

CATH. Right!

She slips out of the jumper.

PHIL. What?

CATH. We've decided.

PHIL. Decided what?

CATH. To go to bed.

PHIL. No, we haven't.

CATH *I* have.

PHIL. I didn't even know that's what we were deciding.

CATH. All right, we'll do it again.

PHIL. And what we're deciding is to go to bed?

CATH. Yes.

PHIL. That's what we've decided to decide?

CATH. Don't start going backwards.

PHIL. Right. We're going to decide to go to bed. Right.

He sits down.

CATH. Oh. You've decided to sit down?

PHIL. No, I've sat down to decide.

She sits beside him.

CATH. So – up we get.

PHIL. Wait! I wasn't ready!

Pause.

CATH. Now?

PHIL. Now.

CATH. Up we get.

PHIL. Up we get.

Pause.

CATH. What's the matter?

PHIL. We haven't got up.

CATH. I'm waiting for you.

PHIL. Try again.

Pause.

CATH. Up we get, then.

PHIL. Up we get. Up we absolutely get.

Pause.

CATH. Now.

PHIL. Now?

CATH. Now.

PHIL. Or now?

CATH. Now!

PHIL. You keep saying different times!

CATH. Look, don't mess around.

She gets up.

PHIL. What?

CATH. I got up.

PHIL. But you didn't *decide* to!

CATH. Yes, I did.

PHIL. You didn't have time.

CATH. I did it simultaneously.

PHIL. No, you didn't. You just got up! Any fool can just *get up*. I could just *get up*.

CATH. You didn't do either.

PHIL. I did! I decided!

CATH. But you didn't get up!

PHIL. No! That's the problem – to combine the two!

CATH. Try tomorrow.

PHIL. No! I'm doing it! I'm doing it now . . .! Don't stand there watching me. I can't do it if you're watching me.

She goes to the mattress, and watches him from there. He closes his eyes.

PHIL. All right, I'm deciding to get up. I'm successfully deciding. I'm gradually successfully deciding . . .

She comes slowly back and stands behind his chair.

Here it comes . . . It's a decision, a successful decision . . . Here it is . . . I've almost successfully decided . . . It's like the sun coming up.

She slowly takes off her jumper.

It's just showing above the horizon now . . . Very bright. I can't look at it. I'm going to sneeze . . .

She wraps her arms round his neck, still holding her jumper. He sniffs it and frowns.

Hold on . . .

She moves away towards the bed. He jumps up.

Cath, that *is* my jumper!

He stops and looks back at where he was sitting.

Oh . . .

Curtain.

ACT TWO

The same.

But the furniture has been rearranged, and the austere order of the first act has become cluttered and confused. The pot plant has grown. The toy dog has disappeared. A battered bicycle with one wheel missing is propped against the wall.

Scene One

CATH is sitting at the table, working. PHIL is sprawling back in the other chair, turned away from the table, holding a vacuum-cleaner and abstractedly picking his nose. He is wearing the same jumper as before, she is not. She suddenly looks up.

CATH. What?

  PHIL *stops picking his nose.*

PHIL. What?

CATH. I thought you said something.

PHIL. No?

CATH. Oh.

  She returns to her work. He returns to his thoughts and his nose.

CATH. There's some soup. It's in the thing.

PHIL. In the thing. Right.

  Pause.

  Isn't there some *soup*?

CATH (*vaguely*). Um.

  Pause.

PHIL. What, in the thing?

  He turns and watches her. She looks up.

CATH. I said there's some *soup*.

PHIL. What do you mean, there's some *soup*? That's what I *said*.
Soup. Isn't there some *soup*? That's what I asked.

CATH. I'm saying yes. Soup. How many times? In the thing.

She goes back to work.

PHIL. I'm talking to myself, am I?

Pause.

CATH. I suppose so . . .

Pause.

PHIL. So where is it, then? In the thing?

Pause. She looks up.

CATH. What?

PHIL. Where is it?

CATH. It's in the thing!

PHIL. In the *thing*. Oh.

CATH. I might as well talk to myself.

*She returns to her work, he to his nose. She looks up and watches him,
frowning. He becomes conscious of her gaze and stops.*

*She returns to her work again, he to his nose. At once she looks up and
watches him expressionlessly. He stops picking his nose, then
demonstratively starts again, looking at her defiantly.*

CATH pushes her books away.

CATH. Go on, then.

PHIL. How do you mean, go on?

CATH. I'm listening.

PHIL. Oh, you're listening now?

CATH. So what do you want to say?

PHIL. What do I want to say?

He thinks.

I don't want to say anything.

CATH. Oh.

PHIL. Why, what do you *want* me to say?

CATH. Whatever you like.

PHIL. Which is nothing.

CATH. All right.

She goes back to work.

PHIL. Or do you mean . . .?

CATH. What?

PHIL. You know.

CATH. No?

PHIL. Yes, you do.

CATH. What?

PHIL. 'I love you.'

CATH. Oh. No. I've given up on that.

PHIL. I've just said it.

CATH. Yes.

PHIL. What?

CATH. Yes! Lovely!

PHIL. Not right?

CATH. No – perfect. Thank you.

PHIL. I can't say it if you say.

CATH. You can't say it if I say and you don't say it if I don't.

PHIL. No. Sad, isn't it.

CATH. Yes.

Pause.

PHIL. Or perhaps you'd like me to say something else?

CATH. All right.

PHIL. What I dreamt about last night?

CATH. If you like.

PHIL. My mother?

CATH. Wonderful.

PHIL. How I felt when I was seventeen? When I'm going to mend the vacuum-cleaner?

CATH. Yes. Yes!

Pause.

You used to say things.

PHIL. Did I?

CATH. Didn't you? We used to sit here and something used to happen.

PHIL. What did I say?

CATH. I can't remember.

PHIL. Lot of good *that* did, then.

CATH. I used to enjoy it.

PHIL. Did you?

CATH. Yes. Didn't you?

Pause.

PHIL. Yes. *You* used to say things.

CATH. I know.

PHIL. What did you say?

CATH. You've forgotten.

PHIL. Yes. So have you.

CATH. No, I haven't.

PHIL. What were they, then?

CATH. Nothing of any importance.

PHIL. Oh.

> *Pause.*

> All right – why don't *you* say something?

CATH. I *am* saying something.

PHIL. What?

CATH. What I'm saying.

PHIL. About why don't I say something?

CATH. Better than sitting here saying nothing.

> *Pause.*

PHIL. Possibly.

> *Pause.*

CATH. You don't notice I'm here half the time.

PHIL. *You* don't notice *I'm* here.

CATH. I notice you picking your nose. You never used to pick your nose when I was here.

PHIL. Yes, I did.

CATH. Only when I wasn't looking.

PHIL. If you weren't looking how did you know I was picking my nose?

> *He gets up and takes the vacuum-cleaner to the alcove. When he returns to the table he is wearing a grinning mask from a novelty shop, and resumes his seat. She works.*

CATH. I don't need to look. I know what you're up to without looking.

Pause.

Anyway, half the time you're *not* here. You're in some world of your own.

Pause.

I know what you're doing now, by the way.

Pause. She glances up, returns to work, then looks up again.

I knew it was something like that.

Pause.

Go on, then.

He waggles his head about.

That's all?

She waggles her head about in imitation.

Oh.

She returns to work. He edges his chair round the table, until he is sitting beside her.

What?

He grins fixedly at her.

I said What?

He moves very slowly closer to her. She leans away from him.

What is it? What do you want?

He brings his face closer to hers.

Don't. I don't like it.

He brings his face closer still.

No!

She turns her head sharply aside.

Pause. They remain immobile, he with his face an inch from hers, she with her face turned aside.

Suddenly he moves back. He takes the mask off, and smiles at her. She turns and watches him.

What was all that about?

PHIL. Surprise.

He leans slowly towards her again, unmasked and smiling. She jumps up and closes her books.

What?

CATH. Surprise.

She goes into the bathroom. The sound of taps running. Pause.

PHIL. So . . . soup. Yes?

Pause. Louder.

I said *Soup*, query.

CATH (*off*). In the bath.

Pause.

(*off*) Did you say what am I doing?

He shakes his head.

(*off*) Can't hear!

He expresses silent surprise and interest.

(*off*) I've told you before . . .

PHIL. . . . you can't hear me when you've got the door shut.

The bathroom door opens, and CATH appears.

CATH. . . . I can't hear you when I've got the door shut! And don't say leave the door open, because I *can't* leave the door open, because if I leave the door open there isn't room to be in there!

She goes back into the bathroom.

PHIL. I'm not saying. Leave the door open . . .

CATH (*off*). And don't say. Then don't be in there!

PHIL. I'm not saying. Don't be in there!

CATH (*off*). Because I've *got* to be in here if I'm going to have a bath . . .!

PHIL. I'm not saying anything.

He picks up the mask and retires to the alcove. He draws the curtain back. It reveals Eric's chair, with books and papers on a small table. He switches on a reading-lamp and sits down.

CATH (*off*). Oh, really . . .? Well, I'm not listening . . .! Wasting your breath . . . La la la la la la la . . .

He pulls the curtain closed. She comes out of the bathroom.

Oh. Though why you're taking refuge in there I don't know, since I'm not in here, I'm in *there*!

She goes back into the bathroom. He looks out from behind the curtain.

PHIL. Why don't you leave the door *half-open*?

The taps are turned off. She comes out of the bathroom, amazed.

CATH. Half-open?

PHIL. Half-open. Yes! Wedge it half-open!

CATH *Half-open*?

PHIL. Half hyphen open.

Pause.

CATH. Half-open . . .

PHIL. Half-open.

He closes the curtain again. She remains where she is.

CATH. I suppose all this is really about . . . well . . .

Pause. He opens the curtain.

PHIL. Really about what?

CATH. You know.

PHIL. No?

CATH. Yes, you do.

PHIL. I haven't the slightest idea what you're talking about.

CATH. I thought I wasn't supposed to say the word?

PHIL. What word?

CATH. Theodore.

Pause. He closes the curtain.

Yes, well, I don't know how we can talk about it if I can't say the name. What's wrong with the name? I don't understand! Theodore . . . Anyway, *you're* the one who put him behind there!

He opens the curtain.

PHIL *I* put him behind here? *I* didn't put him behind here.

CATH. You did!

He comes out of the alcove, pulls the toy dog out from behind the curtain, and whacks it down on to the table.

PHIL *We* put it behind there.

CATH. Oh. Yes. Well . . .

PHIL. You're always doing this.

CATH. Always doing what?

PHIL. Always saying *I* put things somewhere.

CATH. Well, you *did* put this particular thing somewhere!

PHIL. No, I didn't. *We* did!

Pause.

We *did*! We *did*! You're always pretending it's me that makes the decisions.

CATH. Because it *is* you that makes the decisions.

PHIL. It's *us* that make the decisions.

Pause.

CATH. You said We've rather outgrown this kind of thing, haven't we?

PHIL. And you said Yes, we have.

CATH. No, I said If you want to put it behind the thing, then put it behind the thing.

PHIL. Exactly. So then it's me that decided! That's exactly what I'm saying!

CATH. That you decided?

PHIL. That you decided I decided!

CATH. What?

PHIL. Look. I said Do we want to put this thing behind the thing?

CATH. No, *I* said Do *you* want it behind the thing?

PHIL. Would you mind letting me finish?

CATH. Go on.

PHIL. Thank you.

CATH. It was exactly the same with the other thing.

Pause.

PHIL. Am I finishing what I'm saying or aren't I?

CATH. Go on, then.

PHIL. I don't mind waiting while you bring up some other subject first. I just want to know which I'm doing.

CATH. Yes. No. Fine. Get on with it.

PHIL. I'm finishing what I'm saying?

CATH. Yes! Finish what you're saying!

Pause.

PHIL. What do you mean, it was exactly the same with the other thing? What other thing?

CATH. Never mind. Go on.

PHIL. If you mean the bicycle . . .

CATH. No, please. Let's not get back to the bicycle.

PHIL. It wasn't me that brought it up.

CATH. What do you mean, it wasn't you that brought it up?

PHIL. I mean it wasn't me that brought it up!

CATH. Last Saturday!

Pause.

PHIL. Up*stairs*.

CATH. Upstairs, yes!

PHIL. Not up in the conversation.

CATH. What?

PHIL. I didn't bring it up in the conversation.

CATH. In the conversation? No, you brought it up in a towering rage.

PHIL. Anyway . . .

CATH. Anyway . . .

Pause.

PHIL *Our* bicycle, incidentally.

CATH. I *said* 'our bicycle'!

PHIL. You said 'your bicycle'.

CATH. In fact I said 'the bicycle'.

PHIL. You use it just as much as me.

CATH. Yes.

PHIL. You *used* to use it just as much as me.

CATH. However . . .

PHIL. When it had two wheels.

CATH. Let's not talk about the wheels.

PHIL. No.

CATH. So.

PHIL. So.

Pause.

In fact we both know perfectly well what this is all about.

CATH. Do we?

PHIL. It happens every time I go in there.

CATH. Oh, you mean your little hidey-hole?

PHIL. I mean my workspace.

CATH. I mean your workspace.

PHIL. But I thought we'd *agreed*.

CATH. Yes! Fine! Get right back in there and pull the curtain again!

PHIL. What we agreed, if you remember . . .

CATH. I think it's completely mad!

PHIL. Yes, but what we agreed . . .

CATH. But if you can't stand the sight of me then why don't you just move in there for good and never come out?

PHIL. What we agreed . . .

CATH. You and Eric's chair together.

PHIL. What we agreed . . .

CATH. I should have thought it was a little bit *inauthentic*.

PHIL. Never mind inauthentic.

CATH. How about the *natural order?*

PHIL. What?

CATH. The natural order of the universe.

PHIL. I don't know what you're talking about.

CATH. No.

PHIL. What we agreed . . .

Pause.

CATH. Go on, then!

PHIL. Is that we both needed a little personal space.

Pause.

Yes?

CATH. Personal space?

PHIL. Oh, come on.

CATH. Personal space . . .

PHIL. No need to say it like that. They're both perfectly common words. 'Personal' – yes? 'Space' – right?

CATH. Fine. Very . . . authentic.

PHIL. I don't know what you're complaining about.

CATH. I'm not complaining.

PHIL. You've got *your* space.

CATH *My* space?

PHIL. The bathroom!

CATH. The bathroom? *You* use the bathroom!

PHIL. Yes, and *you* can use *my* space!

CATH. Sit behind that curtain? I don't want to sit behind that curtain! I think sitting behind that curtain is about as sane as putting a paper bag over your head and thinking no one can see you!

Pause.

PHIL. Anyway, the relevant fact is that we agreed. Yes?

CATH. Personal space.

PHIL. Just as we also agreed about the bicycle.

CATH. We didn't agree about the bicycle.

PHIL. We agreed that it couldn't stay out on the pavement, because if it did then the other wheel would go as well. Yes?

CATH. I agreed that it couldn't stay on the *pavement* . . .

PHIL. You agreed that it couldn't stay on the *pavement*. Yes. You also agreed . . .

CATH. I didn't agree to keep it in here!

PHIL. You also agreed that it couldn't go in the hall downstairs, or else Pat would fall over it and break her leg, and then she wouldn't be able to come up here and drop in on us at all hours of the day and night, which would be a tragic loss to both of us.

CATH. I didn't agree to keep it in here, though!

PHIL. But there isn't anywhere else!

CATH. So?

PHIL. So, logically . . .

CATH. I thought we agreed you weren't going to say *logically*?

PHIL. Logically . . .

CATH. Let's forget the bicycle.

PHIL. Logically we must have agreed it was coming in here.

CATH. Yes, yes, yes. Fine. Wonderful. Just so long as it's not in *my* bit.

PHIL. All right. Just so long as you agree that we did agree . . .

CATH. Yes. I've said. Yes. So you go back in there, I'll go back in there . . .

She goes to the bathroom. He has not moved.

Now what?

PHIL *Your* bit? What do you mean, *your* bit?

CATH. Round my side of the bed.

PHIL. Oh, that's *your* bit, is it?

CATH *Now* what's going on?

PHIL. I didn't know you had a special bit of the room.

CATH. It's not special. It's simply my side of the bed. What's wrong with that?

PHIL. When was this decided?

CATH. It wasn't decided. It's always been my side of the bed.

PHIL. Always been your side of the bed?

CATH. I thought so.

PHIL. I didn't know that.

CATH. What do you mean, you didn't know that?

PHIL. I mean I didn't know that.

CATH. Personal space.

PHIL. Not in *here*!

CATH. Why not?

PHIL. This is common space! That's the point! Personal space – personal space – common space!

CATH. You've got your bit.

PHIL. No, I haven't.

CATH. Yes, you have.

PHIL. Where?

CATH. Round your side of the bed.

PHIL. This? I don't think of this as my bit.

CATH. Yes, you do.

PHIL. I *do* think of it as my bit?

CATH. Of course you do.

PHIL. How do you know what I think?

CATH. Because if you find anything of mine there you shout What's this thing doing round my side of the bed?

Pause.

PHIL. So where does your bit stop?

CATH. Here.

PHIL. Here. There's a line, is there?

CATH. We don't need a line. We both know.

PHIL. Oh, we both know, do we?

CATH. Of course we know.

PHIL. You mean *you* know?

CATH. I mean we both know.

PHIL. You keep telling me what I know!

CATH. Because you don't seem to know.

PHIL. I don't know what I know?

CATH. Look, I've got things to do.

PHIL. Let me just get this straight. All this is yours? Yes? Over this piece of floor here you have absolute sovereignty. And the boundary of your territory is an imaginary line extending from the foot of the bed. While all *this*, up to an imaginary line from the foot of the bed on this side, is mine, to have and to hold at my own good pleasure, to lease out, sell, burn, put to pasture or develop as building plots, at my own absolute discretion.

CATH. Phil, why are you behaving like this?

PHIL. I'm not behaving like anything. I'm trying, in an absolutely uncontentious way, to codify what seems to have become accepted practice, so that we both know where we stand. Now, these two areas apart, is all the rest of the room subject to mutual agreement or not?

CATH. As far as *I* know.

PHIL. As far as *you* know. Good.

CATH. Well, *isn't* it?

PHIL. As far as *I* know, yes. Though whether I *know* how far I know . . .

CATH. Let's just say yes. Yes, it is.

PHIL. Yes. All right. Yes?

CATH. Yes.

Pause.

Just so long as no more things suddenly vanish behind things.

PHIL. Cath, for the last time!

He snatches up the toy dog.

It wasn't *me* who put this thing behind the thing!

CATH. I know. It was *us*. It's not *you* waving it around. *Us* waving it around. Not *my* face we're waving it in. *Our* face.

PHIL. You *don't* want to talk sensibly – we *won't* talk.

He throws the dog down, returns to the alcove, and draws the curtain. Pause.

CATH. Oh. All right. Fine by me. I'll talk to myself.

She sits down.

Right. Who am I?

Pause.

Anyone else playing? Yes? No . . .? Never mind. So – who am I? Male? Yes. Real? Yes. Human? Half.

Pause.

Someone we both know? Yes. Pat? No – male – I *said.* Someone nice? No. Someone with a foul temper? Yes . . . How many's that?

PHIL (*off*). Seven.

CATH. Seven, right . . . Am I . . . someone who's always trying to talk to people when they're in the bathroom? Yes. Am I . . . someone who screams at people if they leave the bathroom door half-open, then screams at them if they don't? Yes.

Pause.

Someone who always waits for someone else to make up quarrels? Yes. Anyone want to make a guess . . .?

Pause.

PHIL (*off*). Adolf Hitler.

CATH. Right!

She gets up and opens the curtain.

Come on, love . . .

He closes the curtain.

CATH. Oh, stay in there, then! Stay in there for good! Don't come out at all!

She goes back towards the bathroom, then changes her mind and goes out of the front door. Pause. PHIL opens the curtain and looks out. He reluctantly emerges and crosses to the bathroom door.

PHIL. Sorry.

Pause. Louder.

Sorry!

Pause.

Cath . . .?

Pause.

You haven't got the taps on, don't pretend you can't hear . . . I'm not going to play silly games . . . I've said I'm sorry . . .

Pause.

All right, then – who am I?

Pause.

Am I female? Yes, I am.

Pause.

I know you're listening – I can hear you . . . I can hear you *listening*? – Yes. – How can I hear you listening? – I have very sharp ears.

Pause.

All right. Someone we like? Someone *I* like. Quite like. Some of the time. When she's not doing this kind of thing. What kind of thing? *That* kind of thing! Exactly! Pretending she doesn't know what I mean when I say *This* kind of thing . . . Queen Victoria? No . . . Someone who's always saying I never say I love her, only I do, I'm always saying it, it's just she never notices, in fact I'm saying it now, and she's not even replying . . .

Pause.

Cath, come *on*! Don't be like that! *I* said something! I said I was Hitler!

Pause.

You're always saying *I* sulk, *I* won't make up quarrels . . .

Pause. CATH *pushes open the front door, and stops at the sight of him.*

So I'm just standing here talking to myself, am I?

CATH. Apparently.

Pause.

PHIL. Oh. Very clever.

CATH. What?

PHIL. You were listening, were you?

CATH. Listening? No? Listening to what?

PHIL. Nothing.

CATH. Listening to nothing?

PHIL. Never mind.

CATH. Why, what were you saying?

PHIL. Nothing at all.

CATH. Something I wasn't supposed to hear?

PHIL. No.

CATH. No you weren't? Or no I wasn't?

PHIL. I'm not going to say it again.

CATH. Not going to say what again?

PHIL. Nothing.

Pause.

CATH. Oh.

She goes to the bathroom.

PHIL. Cath!

CATH. What?

Pause.

What?

PHIL. How's it all got like this?

CATH. Like what?

PHIL. All so . . . like this!

CATH. Yes . . .

PHIL. It usen't to be like this!

CATH. Usen't it?

PHIL. No!

CATH. I can't remember.

PHIL. Cath!

CATH. Well . . . things change.

PHIL. What things?

CATH. Things.

PHIL. You mean me?

CATH. No.

PHIL. You?

CATH. Possibly.

PHIL. You haven't changed.

CATH. Haven't I?

PHIL. Have you?

CATH. I don't know.

PHIL. I'll tell you what's changed. It's not me. It's not you. It's us.

CATH. No!

PHIL. No?

CATH. Don't say things like that.

PHIL. If they're true . . .

CATH. Don't say them.

PHIL. No . . .

CATH. Anyway, it's this place.

PHIL. What – changed?

CATH. No, *not* changed! *Not* changed, that's the trouble! It's all this! And this! And this!

PHIL. I thought you liked this place?

CATH. I do!

PHIL. You used to like it.

CATH. I do like it! I just want to . . .

PHIL. What?

CATH. Get out of here!

PHIL. Move?

CATH. Not move.

PHIL. Go away?

CATH. For a bit. Yes? Get right away from it all.

PHIL. All right. The question is when.

CATH. When?

PHIL. When we can get away.

CATH. Now!

PHIL. What – this week?

CATH. No! Now!

She opens the door.

Come on!

PHIL. Cath, don't play games.

CATH. I'm not playing games.

PHIL. I hate it when you play games.

CATH. All we've got to do is walk out of the door.

PHIL. Except we can't.

CATH. Why not?

PHIL. We've got things to do.

CATH. Forget them.

PHIL. Your thing.

CATH. What thing?

PHIL. I don't know. Your thing tomorrow.

CATH. Oh, that.

PHIL. You see?

CATH. We'll forget about it. Come on! Off we go.

She waits, holding the door open.

PHIL. We could go for a walk.

CATH. We could go anywhere.

PHIL. Where's anywhere?

CATH. Anywhere we like.

PHIL. We can't go *anywhere*. We've got to go *somewhere*.

CATH. China?

PHIL. Cath!

CATH. That's somewhere.

PHIL. Yes.

CATH. Bournemouth.

PHIL. Wonderful. What, without packing?

CATH. What do we need?

PHIL. All kinds of things.

CATH. This?

PHIL. Not that.

CATH. This? This? This?

PHIL. Jumpers.

CATH. You've got your jumper.

PHIL. We could go to your mother's . . .

CATH. Anywhere.

PHIL. Anywhere. All right. How about . . . here?

CATH. Here?

PHIL. Here's anywhere.

Pause.

CATH. Here . . .

She closes the door.

All right. Here.

PHIL. Do you mind?

CATH. Not at all.

PHIL. Even if we'd gone somewhere else, it would still have been here when we'd got there.

CATH. Yes. So, here we are.

PHIL. Here we are.

She looks round the room.

CATH. What do you think?

PHIL. What?

CATH. Quite nice. Rather like home. Have we got a view?

She looks out of the window.

PHIL. No games, though, Cath.

CATH. Why not? We're on holiday . . . Bit of a view.

PHIL. Let's just *be*. All right?

CATH. Bathroom?

PHIL. Cath!

She looks into the bathroom.

CATH. Yes. They've even run the bath for us.

PHIL. It's just so exhausting when you start all this kind of thing.

He hurls himself down on to the bed.

CATH. What's the bed like?

PHIL. I'm not playing.

She sits down on one of the chairs.

Pause.

What are you doing now?

CATH. Nothing.

PHIL. Nothing. Good.

CATH. Having a holiday. Relaxing. Watching the world go by.

Pause.

Why? What are you doing?

PHIL. Nothing.

CATH. Relaxing?

PHIL. No.

CATH. Not relaxing?

PHIL. No.

CATH. Close your eyes.

PHIL. I don't want to close my eyes. I don't want to do anything.

CATH. So what are you looking at?

PHIL. The ceiling.

CATH. What's it like?

PHIL. What's it like? The ceiling? It's not like anything.

CATH. Not like a ceiling?

Pause.

PHIL. Yes, it's like a ceiling. That's exactly what it's like. A ceiling.

Pause.

CATH. Any frescoes on it?

PHIL. Cath . . .

CATH. What?

PHIL. Don't.

CATH. Don't what?

PHIL. Don't anything. All right? Don't make things any worse.

Pause.

CATH. Not overdoing it, are you?

PHIL. What?

CATH. Not getting too much sun?

Pause.

PHIL. I'm not getting too much sun, no.

CATH. Or bitten by anything?

Pause.

PHIL. Not bitten.

CATH. Perfect place.

PHIL. Cath, I'm so miserable!

Pause.

CATH. Phil . . .

PHIL. Nothing else!

CATH. I love you.

Pause.

PHIL. Yes.

CATH. Yes?

PHIL. I know.

CATH. Oh, you know?

PHIL. You know I know.

CATH. How do you know?

PHIL. I just do.

CATH. Because I say it.

PHIL. Because you don't need to say it.

Pause.

Anyway I said it.

CATH. Said what?

PHIL. The converse.

CATH. When?

PHIL. Earlier.

CATH. Oh, then.

PHIL. You see?

CATH. You just said the words.

PHIL. Not then.

CATH. You didn't mean the meaning.

PHIL. Not then.

CATH. So when?

PHIL. Another time.

CATH. I didn't hear it.

PHIL. No, you weren't there.

Pause.

CATH. Oh. So what did you say?

PHIL. You know what I said.

CATH. Go on.

PHIL. Not now you've said Say it.

CATH. I didn't say Say it! I most carefully didn't say Say it! I said Go on!

PHIL. Yes, but it would still be . . .

CATH. Still be what? What would it be, as a matter of interest?

PHIL. Inauthentic.

She runs over to the bed and jumps on top of him.

CATH. Phil, I'm going to kill you!

PHIL. All right. Good idea. Only not . . . agh!

CATH. Not what?

PHIL. That way.

CATH. What way?

PHIL. By crushing my . . . agh!

CATH. What, this?

PHIL. Yes!

CATH. Oh, yes . . . Yes . . . What's happening?

PHIL. What do you mean, what's happening?

CATH. I think it's trying to tell us something.

PHIL. No, it's not.

CATH. What's it saying?

PHIL. It's not saying anything.

CATH. Yes, it is.

PHIL. Yes, because you're making it.

CATH. I'm saying Say it?

PHIL. Yes!

CATH. Oh. So its response is . . .?

PHIL. Exactly!

CATH. What?

PHIL. I'm not saying the word again.

CATH. Come on. Its response is . . .?

He rolls her over and gets on top of her.

PHIL. Disconcertingly authentic.

A knock at the door.

PAT (*off*). Cath . . .

They stop.

CATH. Hello?

PHIL (*whispers*). She listens! She waits outside that door and listens!

CATH (*whispers*). Actually . . .

PHIL (*whispers*). Oh, no!

CATH (*whispers*). I said if she felt like it . . .

PHIL (*whispers*). You went down?

CATH (*whispers*). You were behind there!

PHIL (*whispers*). I thought we'd *agreed*?

PAT (*off*). Cath . . .?

CATH. Coming! (*Whispers.*) Get off!

He lets her get up.

PHIL (*whispers*). We *agreed*!

CATH (*whispers*). I'll get rid of her.

PAT (*off*). Cath, I'll come back.

CATH. Hold on!

She goes to the door. He retires to the alcove.

(*whispers*) You're not . . .?

PHIL (*whispers*). I am.

CATH (*whispers*). You can't!

PHIL (*whispers*). I can.

He closes the curtain. She opens the door.

PAT. What – trouble?

CATH. No. Come in.

PAT comes uncertainly in.

PAT. Only I don't want to come up if it's the wrong moment . . .

CATH. It's not. Sit down.

PAT. He's out, is he?

CATH. No. Tea? Coffee?

PAT. Not for me, love.

She sits down.

What, he's in the . . .?

She nods at the bathroom.

CATH. No, no.

PAT. Oh, sorry. Only I thought . . .

CATH. Of course.

PAT looks round the room. She lowers her voice.

PAT. He's not behind the . . .?

CATH. Yes.

PAT. Oh, I see.

Pause.

CATH. Phil?

Pause.

Phil!

PAT. Yes, well, don't bother him, Cath.

CATH. Phil!

PHIL (*off*). What?

CATH. Pat's here.

Pause.

PHIL (*off*). Hello.

PAT *stands up.*

PAT. I'll come back another time, Cath.

CATH. Sit down.

PAT. He's got things to do.

CATH. Has he?

PAT. You've both got things to do, I know that.

CATH. No, no.

She straightens the bedclothes.

PAT. I wouldn't have come, only you said . . .

CATH. Yes!

PAT. And I thought Lovely, and then I thought No, hold on, don't rush at it, I know Phil doesn't want me up there all the time . . .

CATH. Don't be silly.

PAT. And now of course things have moved on, I know how it is . . .

CATH. Just sit down. Don't take any notice.

PAT *sits down at the table.* CATH *sits opposite her. Pause.*

PAT. So it came in handy in the end, then?

CATH. What?

PAT. Eric's chair.

CATH. Oh, yes.

PAT. Didn't like the look of it, did he? Now he's in there sitting on it.

CATH. Yes.

PAT. Funny how it all works out, isn't it.

CATH. Quite funny.

PAT. Eric was like that. He'd go all quiet, not a word out of him. He'd come up here, you know. Get away from me. Then nothing. Just cough cough.

CATH. Yes, Phil thinks we all have to have this . . . personal space. (*Louder*). Personal space – yes?

They both look at the curtain. No response.

PAT. Well, you've got to get out of each other's way, Cath. I don't know where *you* go off to.

CATH. Me? Nowhere.

PHIL (*off*). The bathroom.

CATH. Oh, yes, the bathroom. The bathroom's me. Except when he's using it, which is at least as often as me. And then I have this piece of floor here, running up to an imaginary line extending from the foot of the bed.

PAT. No, but you do, don't you. You divide things up.

CATH. This is him, here, up to an imaginary line on this side of the bed.

PAT. I was the windows. Anything to do with the windows – that was me. He always blamed me for the windows. So that was *my* fault, of course, when the sash broke, and the window came down on top of him.

CATH *He's* the windows. I'm the curtains.

PAT. No, I was always the windows. Windows and door-handles. And the roof. And the fireplaces. Because he liked modern, you see, Eric. He was always for modern. So anything that wasn't modern in the house, and it went wrong, that was my fault. He'd sit there reading his paper and I'd know something was up just from the look on his face. So I wouldn't say anything – I wouldn't give him the satisfaction. I'd wait. He'd go on reading the paper, not a word, just this tight little look, and I'd know he'd got this wonderful grievance. I'd wait. *He'd* wait. Then just as I was going out of the room, say, just as I was putting the supper on the table, out it would bounce. 'The bedroom door-handle,' he'd say. It used to make me so cross! 'The bedroom door-handle.' Like that. As soon as he said it I could feel my muscles all clench up. I'd just stop where I was, look at him, wait, not say anything. 'It's loose, it's going to come off,' he'd say. And so pleased with himself! Always knew I'd got a bad character, and now here I was, caught in the act, letting the bedroom door-handle get loose. So of course I wouldn't admit it. Nothing to do with me! 'Oh,' I'd say, 'is it really? Then why don't you get upstairs and mend it?' But inside, Cath, inside, I knew he was right, I knew it was me that had done it, because if it was the door-handle then it had to be me. So he wouldn't mend it, and I wouldn't get Mr Weeks to do it, and he'd sigh and raise his eyebrows every time he put his hand on it, and not say anything, and I'd look the other way, and not say anything, until in the end it'd fall off, and then at last, with a special holy look like Jesus picking up the cross, he'd get the toolbox out, and there wouldn't be any screws in the tin, so he'd have to do it with three nails and some glue instead, and there'd be blood dripping on the carpet, only he wouldn't let me put a plaster on it for him, and then I *couldn't* tell Mr Weeks about it when he came to do the boiler because that'd look as if I was criticising his handiwork and turning up my nose at the great sacrifice he'd made even though he was in the right and I was in the wrong.

Pause.

The boiler, that was me as well.

CATH. I'm the soap, I don't know why.

PAT. The boiler, the drain outside the back door. Yes, I don't know why I was the drain.

CATH. The soap and the towels.

PAT. But then *he* was the lights and the washing-machine. Oh yes. All the machines, all the electrical. Anything modern, you see. He'd come home in the evening – darkness. 'That washing machine,' I'd say before he could so much as open his mouth. 'You'll have to do something about it, Eric. Water all over the floor. Flash! Crack! I wonder it didn't kill me.' And at once he'd go mad. 'There's nothing wrong with the machine,' he'd say. 'It's what you ask it to do.' Shouting away at me. Because he knew it was his fault, you see, the washing-machine. If it was a gadget, if it was labour-saving, then that was his responsibility. Poor Eric. Poor old boy. But you can't take the blame for everything, can you, Cath. You've got to divide things up.

CATH. My relations.

PAT. Oh, relations, yes. All down to you. All *his* relations.

CATH. All our friends.

PAT. People. Other people. That's all your side of the business.

CATH. 'You haven't invited so-and-so round again?'

PAT. That's me, is it?

CATH. Not you. No.

PAT. I bet it is. You'd be down to me if Eric was here.

Pause.

Is he all right behind there?

CATH. I expect so.

PAT. We're not disturbing him?

CATH. No. He's disturbing us.

Pause.

PAT. Anything to do with strikes, trains not running, traffic-jams, that kind of thing, that was modern, that was Eric's fault. Football hooligans. Russia. Oh, yes, he was always Labour. America. Yes, well – modern again.

Pause.

Yes, and it was the same with the children. If David did anything wrong, that was me. If it was Peter it was him, only of course if it was Peter it wasn't wrong, he wouldn't hear of it. I don't know about Lucy. He thought Lucy was me, I thought she was him, so she got it both ways, poor kid, she got it coming and going. Now she lives in a tip – I wouldn't stable a horse in there. No, all kinds of things you're going to find out about each other as soon as there are three of you. You'll be off out of here by then, though. I'll have two more faces in here. Two more strangers.

PHIL *opens the curtain. He has his back towards the room as he picks up his chair.*

Oh, here he is. That's right, fetch your chair, come and talk to us.

PHIL *sets the chair at the table between* CATH *and* PAT, *and sits down. He is wearing the mask again.*

Oh, no! What's all this?

PHIL *looks from one to the other, grinning.*

What's he up to, Cath?

CATH. I've no idea.

PAT. Some kind of performance?

CATH. I expect so.

PHIL *waggles his head, but says nothing.*

What were we talking about?

PAT. Yes, what were we talking about?

PHIL *takes an intelligent interest in the conversation, turning from one to the other as he waits for* PAT *to speak.*

CATH. Dividing things up.

PAT. Yes.

CATH. The children.

PAT. That's right.

CATH. Go on about the children.

PAT. I must be getting back, Cath.

She rises.

CATH. Sit down.

PAT. I've got the washing-machine on . . .

CATH. Sit down!

PAT *sits. Pause.*

The children . . .

PAT. No, but it's funny, though.

CATH. What?

PAT. That chair. How things change.

CATH. Yes.

Pause. PAT *sees the toy dog.*

PAT. Oh, and Theodore's come out again! He used to be up there, do you remember?

CATH. Yes.

PAT. Been everywhere, that dog. In, out, up, down. Wonderful, the use you've got out of him.

CATH. Wonderful.

PAT. I remember when you first saw this place. 'No! No!' You remember that, Cath?

CATH. Yes.

Pause.

PAT. Now here you are.

CATH. Here we are.

Pause.

I'm sorry.

PAT. No. Lovely smile.

Pause.

CATH. Yes.

She goes out to the bathroom. Pause.

PAT. What, I walked into the middle of one, did I?

Pause. PHIL *takes off the mask.*

Knew I had, soon as I came through the door.

PHIL (*indicates the mask*). It was a little surprise for her.

PAT. Oh, I see. That what *I* am?

PHIL. What?

PAT. Her little surprise for you?

Pause.

PHIL. We *weren't* having a row. As it happens.

PAT *We'd* have rows. Eric and me. He'd get so angry! The angrier he got the less he'd say. The less he said the more I said. The more I said the angrier he got. Round and round. Up and down. Back and forth. Soon as it stops – up it starts again. Then afterwards – you can't even remember what it was all about.

PHIL. What was the rest of it about?

PAT. What rest of it?

PHIL. When you weren't having rows.

PAT. Oh, then.

PHIL. You remember that?

PAT. What it was about?

PHIL. What it was like.

PAT. It wasn't like anything, my love. Just there it was.

PHIL. Yes.

PAT. There it was. Then there it wasn't. It doesn't last long, Phil, I'll tell you that, whatever it's like.

She picks up the alarm-clock from the shelf where it's now standing.

Tick tock, says Mr Clock.

She goes to the front door.

One moment it's there, and it's there forever. Next moment . . . (*Calls*) Cath! Cath, love . . .!

PHIL *turns to look at the bathroom door. When he turns back* PAT *has gone out of the front door.*

PHIL. Tick tock.

The bathroom door opens and CATH *comes out.*

CATH. Gone?

PHIL. Gone.

She sits down at the table and resumes her work.

Tick tock.

CATH. What?

PHIL. Nothing.

Pause.

We were on the bed. Do you remember?

CATH. Yes.

PHIL. Tick tock. Tick tock.

Pause.

In the thing?

CATH. What?

PHIL. The soup.

CATH. Yes.

Pause.

PHIL. Quick bath.

CATH. Yes.

PHIL. You didn't have a bath.

CATH. No.

PHIL. Water's cold?

CATH. Yes.

PHIL. Everything gets cold. The water. The soup.

Pause. He picks up the alarm-clock and examines it.

CATH. What?

PHIL. Tick tock.

CATH. What about it?

PHIL. Time.

CATH. Yes.

PHIL. It's going.

CATH. I know.

He sits down at the table with the alarm-clock, studying it. Pause.

PHIL. Round it goes. Down . . . down . . . Under . . . Up the other side . . .

CATH. I've told you – it's in the thing.

PHIL. Up it goes. Up . . . up . . . Up and over . . .

CATH. Get it yourself, if you want to eat.

PHIL. This is fascinating. It goes quite slowly when you look at it. Much more slowly than you'd have thought. No hurry at all. Round it comes again . . . Oh, this isn't so bad after all. This is really quite reassuring. Look . . .

CATH. Yes.

PHIL. You're not looking.

CATH. I looked.

PHIL. You have to keep looking.

CATH. Lovely.

PHIL. Keep your eyes on it.

CATH. I've got work to do. I've got my thing tomorrow.

PHIL. You'll see how slowly tomorrow's coming. You'll get a pleasant surprise.

Pause.

I've got a thing tomorrow. That doesn't stop me doing things today . . .

Looks at the clock.

Look at it. On it goes. On and on. Taking it as it comes. A moment at a time. Living every minute to the full.

CATH *You've* got a thing tomorrow?

PHIL. Of course.

Pause.

What thing have I got tomorrow?

CATH. You're asking me?

PHIL. You don't know.

CATH. You haven't got a thing tomorrow.

PHIL. I've got a thing tomorrow.

CATH. I don't know what you're talking about.

PHIL. No, we don't seem to speak the same language any more.

CATH. A thing?

PHIL. You don't know what the word means.

Pause.

You always used to know.

Pause.

We both always used to know.

CATH. Yes.

She pushes her work aside, and looks at the clock.

PHIL. You see? Down . . . down . . . Nice and slow.

CATH. I don't call that slow.

PHIL. Slow and steady.

CATH. It's quite fast. I call that fast.

PHIL. Still coming down . . . Not halfway round yet . . .

CATH. It is now.

PHIL. Oh, *now* it is.

CATH. Now it's past halfway.

PHIL. It's on the seven.

CATH. It's past the seven . . . It's nearly on the eight . . .

PHIL. It's on the eight.

CATH. It's past the eight . . .

PHIL. Up it goes. Up . . . up . . .

CATH. You can't take it in. It keeps changing. Every time you think you know where it is it's somewhere else.

PHIL. Ten . . .

CATH. If it just stopped there for a moment . . . Or there . . .

PHIL. Eleven . . .

CATH. I'm trying to imagine it stopped . . . There . . . No – there . . .

PHIL. Twelve . . .

CATH. Close your eyes.

PHIL. It's coming down again.

CATH. Close your eyes!

PHIL. Five . . . Closing our eyes won't stop it.

CATH. Yes, it will.

PHIL. Ten . . .

CATH. Just do it. All right? Now, have we both got our eyes closed?

PHIL. Yes.

CATH. Yes?

PHIL. Yes. Twenty . . .

CATH. Come on.

PHIL. OK. It's still going round, though.

CATH. We don't know what it's doing.

PHIL. Yes, we do.

CATH. Not if we've got our eyes shut.

PHIL. Cath!

CATH. What?

PHIL. You're being all like that again.

CATH. No, I'm not. It might have stopped.

PHIL. It hasn't stopped.

CATH. We don't know.

PHIL. I've just looked.

CATH. Well, don't look.

PHIL. Cath, you're driving me mad!

CATH. Eyes closed.

PHIL. Oh, not again.

CATH. We haven't done it yet.

PHIL. Done what?

CATH. You'll see.

PHIL. Not with my eyes closed I won't.

CATH. Are they closed?

PHIL. Yes! Come on. Let's get on with it.

CATH. Now, when I say 'open', open them. Yes? And when I say
    'shut', shut them. All right?

PHIL. This is ridiculous.

CATH. Ready?

PHIL. No.

CATH. Open. Shut.

PHIL. What?

CATH. Open . . .

PHIL. Hold on.

CATH. Open. Shut.

PHIL. I can't shut them before I've got them open!

CATH. Open. Shut.

PHIL *I'll* say it. Open. Shut.

CATH. We'll both say it.

PHIL. ⎫
CATH. ⎭ (*together*) Open. Shut.

PHIL. Again.

PHIL. ⎫
CATH. ⎭ (*together*) Open. Shut.

CATH. You see?

PHIL. See what?

CATH. We caught it!

PHIL. Caught what?

CATH. The thing. We caught it not moving!

PHIL. Oh, the thing.

CATH. You weren't looking at the thing?

PHIL. I was looking at you.

CATH. Oh. Was *I* moving?

PHIL. No.

CATH. What was I doing?

PHIL. Nothing. You were just . . . Hold on, I'll do it again. You were just . . . Open. Shut . . . Just *there*.

CATH. Just *there*?

PHIL. Do it to me. We'll do it to each other. Eyes closed . . .

CATH. What are we trying to do?

PHIL. To get hold of it all for a moment. To see what we're like *now*.

CATH. Now?

PHIL *Now*!

CATH. Are we saying 'now' or are we saying 'open'?

PHIL. We're saying 'now'.

CATH. 'Now.' Right.

PHIL. We'll say it together.

CATH. When?

PHIL. When?

PHIL.   } (*together*) *Now!*
CATH.

PHIL. Brilliant!

They both open their eyes permanently.

CATH. You had your eyes wide open!

PHIL. So did you! And your mouth!

CATH. Yes! You had your mouth open!

PHIL. We'll always remember that.

CATH. When we're very old.

PHIL. And everything's got mixed up in our memory and run together with everything else . . .

CATH. And we can't remember what anything was like . . .

PHIL. We'll remember that once . . .

CATH. Once . . .

PHIL. At one particular moment in time . . .

CATH. It was now . . .

PHIL. Precisely now, and we were precisely like that.

CATH. Yes. Like what?

PHIL. That.

CATH. With our eyes open?

PHIL. Yes.

CATH. And our mouths?

PHIL. Yes!

CATH. Yes. Yes . . .

PHIL. What?

CATH. Not *just* with our mouths open.

PHIL. No.

CATH. With all the things we were thinking as well, all the things we were feeling.

PHIL. Yes! No.

CATH. No?

PHIL. There wasn't time to be thinking or feeling. Not in that instant.

CATH *I* was thinking.

PHIL. Not in that *instant*, you weren't.

CATH. Yes, I was.

PHIL. You couldn't have been.

CATH. I *was*!

PHIL. What were you thinking?

CATH. Never mind.

PHIL. Oh, I see. Yes. Well.

CATH. I know *you* weren't.

PHIL. No, because I couldn't. By the time I'd have thought 'I' the instant would have been over. There wouldn't have been time to get on to the 'love', never mind the 'you'.

CATH. No.

PHIL. Well, there wouldn't.

CATH. No.

PHIL. What you mean is that you thought it just afterwards.

CATH. That's not what I mean.

PHIL. You mean you realised just afterwards that this was what you had been in the process of thinking at the time.

CATH. You don't know what I mean.

PHIL. I know what you *don't* mean.

CATH. And you don't know what I was thinking.

PHIL. I know what you *weren't* thinking, because I know what you *can't* have been thinking, and I know you *can't* have been thinking it because *logically* . . .

CATH. Logically?

PHIL *Logically*, yes.

CATH. Logically . . .

PHIL *Logically*, *logically*. And don't tell me I'm not allowed to say *logically* – you're always telling me what I'm allowed to say and what I'm not allowed to say, and if *logically* is what I think, then *logically* is what I'm going to say . . .

She puts on the mask.

Oh, very funny.

She waggles her head, but says nothing.

Yes, but *I* didn't do it in the middle of a serious conversation.

She cocks her head quizzically.

I don't know what all this is about. I thought we were getting on, I thought we were friends . . .?

She nods.

I put it on to *amuse* you, not to get out of an argument . . . It doesn't make any difference. I know what's going on inside your head even if you put a bucket over it . . . What's *not* going on. What *can't* be going on. Logically.

She moves very slowly closer to him. He leans away from her.

What?

She brings her face closer to his.

No. Frankly.

Pause. They remain immobile, she with her face an inch from his, he with his face turned aside. Then she straightens up. He gets to his feet.

Personal space. Remember?

He goes to the alcove and draws the curtain. She waits, grinning, then takes off the mask. She looks at the clock.

CATH. Up . . . up . . . over the top . . . down . . . down . . . You're not working, you know. You're just sitting there . . . I know what you're thinking. You're thinking: 'I'm not just sitting here, as a matter of fact – I'm working.' But you can never work if you're in a temper. So now you're thinking: 'I'm not in a temper . . .!' You know what else you're doing? You're picking your nose . . . Only now I've said it you've stopped . . . And now I've said that you've started again . . . Round the corner it goes . . . Round and up. Up . . . up . . . I *was* thinking it, you know. I'll tell you how I know I was thinking it. Because I think it all the time. I don't have to think the words, one by one. The thought's just in my mind, complete, every moment of the day. Even now. Especially now . . . Over the top again. Another minute gone . . . What are you doing now? You're listening. You're thinking 'Shall I come out?' 'No,' you're thinking, 'I'd better sulk for a bit longer. Then I'll come out, and I won't say anything, but I'll give her a little kiss on the back of her neck, and I'll put the soup on the table, and we'll eat, and we'll talk, and we'll go to bed, and we'll put our arms round each other, and everything will be all right.'

She looks at the clock.

It's still *now* . . . Now . . . Now . . . More now . . . Or perhaps you're thinking something else altogether. I don't know. Perhaps you're not thinking. Not breathing . . . I don't know, do I, if I can't see you . . . Can't touch you, can't hear you . . . I don't even know if you exist . . . Not *logically*. Do I . . .? Perhaps you don't exist. Perhaps you never did exist . . . Phil . . .? Love . . .?

She goes to the curtain across the alcove.

Phil . . .?

Pause. She comes back to the table and stands at it, uneasy, head half-turned towards the alcove.

Phil!

She runs back to the alcove and pulls open the curtain. He is not there. She stands still for a moment, then pulls the curtain fully open. It reveals nothing but all the stuff they have stored there. She pulls odd pieces out. There is nowhere he could be hiding. She looks round the room, trying to think calmly. Then she flings the bedclothes aside.

Phil, come on!

She looks wildly into the bathroom, even opens the kitchenette.

Don't be silly . . . I know you're there . . . I can see you . . .!

She waits. Nothing. She begins to panic. She looks in all the same places again, then drags the curtain back to its original position and starts to search the alcove from the opposite end.

Phil, please! Please . . .! Please . . .! Please . . .!

She runs to the front door and opens it.

Pat . . .!

She stops, thinks again, holding her head.

No . . .

She closes the door and takes a hold on herself. She goes back to the curtain, and pulls it slowly and methodically aside. PHIL is sitting at his desk, working. At the sight of her he pushes his books aside and emerges.

PHIL. Did you say soup?

She looks at him.

CATH. Soup. Yes.

She reaches out and touches him.

PHIL. What?

CATH. Nothing.

PHIL. In the thing?

CATH. In the thing.

He picks up the toy dog, tosses it behind the curtain, then crosses to the kitchenette and starts to heat the soup.

Blackout.

Scene Two

Half the pictures are off the wall, half the books off the shelves, stacked ready for moving. Half the contents of the room have either already gone, or are in plastic bin-liners. CATH is throwing things into a bin-liner. PHIL is standing holding the pillows.

CATH. What?

PHIL. Nothing. Just looking.

CATH. Looking at what?

PHIL. All this.

CATH. Rubbish.

PHIL. Rubbish?

CATH. This.

She drags the bin-liner to the door, and continues to work.

Phil, don't just stand there!

PHIL. I'm not just standing there.

CATH. You're not *doing* anything.

PHIL. I *am* doing something.

CATH. Carry some stuff down to the van.

PHIL. I'm feeling.

CATH. Feeling? Feeling what?

PHIL. You know . . . Just a bit . . . Well . . .

CATH. Oh. Yes. Bed.

She starts to strip the bed.

PHIL. I mean, just a bit. Aren't you?

CATH. Yes. Come on.

He puts the pillows into the rubbish-bag.

PHIL. You're not.

CATH. I am. Bed, bed!

He helps her strip the bed.

PHIL. Remember the snowstorm?

CATH. What did you do with the pillows?

PHIL. Bag. And we were rolling off the edge of the world?

CATH. That's rubbish!

She takes the pillows out of the rubbish-bag and transfers them to another bin-liner.

PHIL. And Pat came in?

She indicates different bin-liners.

CATH. Rubbish . . . Bedroom . . . Living-room . . . Right?

PHIL. Right. She thought I was murdering you. Do you remember that?

CATH. Yes. Up . . .

They up-end the mattress.

PHIL. Heartbreaking.

CATH. What's the matter?

PHIL. It took us two years to get it there.

CATH. Ready?

PHIL. First we had it *there*. No, first we had it *there*! I'd forgotten that.

CATH. Lift . . .

PHIL. Now . . .

CATH. Move . . .

They carry the mattress to the door.

PHIL. . . . nowhere.

CATH. Mind the thing.

PHIL. So slow to put things together . . .

They carry the mattress out.

(*off*) Down the stairs?

CATH (*off*). Over the bannisters.

PHIL (*off*). Over the bannisters?

CATH (*off*). Quicker.

The sound of the mattress falling down the stairwell. They reappear.

PHIL. So quick to blow them all to bits again . . .

He looks back at the door, hand to mouth.

Pat!

CATH. She went to the corner. Get that thing out of the way.

She indicates the plant.

PHIL. You remember the size it was when we bought it?

CATH. Yes.

He starts to slide it towards the door, while she goes on clearing the room.

PHIL. You wanted to put it in the corner there.

CATH. Anyway, it'll get plenty of light in the new living-room.

He stops work.

PHIL. The living-room?

CATH. Presumably.

PHIL. Oh.

CATH. It's not going in the bedroom?

PHIL. Isn't it?

CATH. Is it?

PHIL. It's always *been* in the bedroom.

CATH. What, this? This wasn't the bedroom.

PHIL. This wasn't the bedroom?

CATH. Yes, well, now we've got a living-room *and* a bedroom we've got to decide about things.

PHIL. So what are you saying?

CATH. What do you mean, what am I saying? I'm saying get the plant out of here before someone falls over it.

PHIL. You're saying you don't like it?

CATH. I love it!

PHIL. You don't.

CATH. All right, I don't.

PHIL. You *don't* like it?

CATH. I just don't want it in my bedroom.

PHIL *Your* bedroom?

CATH *The* bedroom.

PHIL *Our* bedroom.

She holds up something.

CATH. This thing?

PHIL. Cath, we're not going to let it take over, are we, having a bedroom and a living-room? We're not going to let it change us?

CATH. No. Do we want to keep it?

PHIL. No.

She dumps it in the rubbish-bag.

PHIL. Yes.

CATH. Make up your mind.

She takes it out of the rubbish-bag.

PHIL. Make up *my* mind?

CATH. Make up *our* mind.

PHIL. Right.

CATH. No.

She dumps it in the rubbish-bag.

PHIL. Cath, what is all this?

CATH. What is all what?

PHIL. All this great thing.

CATH. I just want to get on, get out of here.

PHIL. Get out of here?

CATH. Now we're going.

PHIL. I thought you liked this place.

CATH. So you keep saying.

PHIL. And you don't?

CATH. I *did*.

PHIL *Did?*

CATH. Come on! We've got to get things done!

They begin sliding the plant out of the room.

PHIL. So when did you stop liking the *plant*?

CATH. I've never liked it.

PHIL *Never* liked it?

He stops work.

CATH. Not much, no.

PHIL. Not when we bought it?

CATH. No.

PHIL. We bought it together! We chose it together!

CATH *You* chose it.

She drags the plant out single-handed. He follows her out.

PHIL (*off*). What are you saying?

CATH (*off*). Don't keep saying what am I saying! I'm saying what I'm saying!

She comes back in, and sets to work on the pictures. He follows her back in.

PHIL. You said you liked it.

CATH. When?

PHIL. When we bought it.

CATH. Did I?

PHIL. Why did you say you liked it if you didn't?

CATH. No idea. Are we taking this?

She holds up one of the pictures.

PHIL. Are we taking *that*? What's happening?

CATH. Yes or no?

PHIL. You don't like *that*, either?

CATH. I love it.

PHIL. I don't understand . . .

CATH. You want it?

PHIL *I* want it.

CATH. Then we're taking it.

She puts it and other pictures outside the door.

PHIL. How about the table?

CATH. Table. Right.

She picks up one end, and waits for him to pick up the other.

PHIL. You want to take it?

CATH. Do I want to take the *table*?

PHIL. Yes.

CATH. Don't mess around.

PHIL. No, I'm asking you.

CATH. Yes. I want to take the table.

PHIL. You like the table?

CATH. I can't lift it on my own.

PHIL. I want to know.

Pause.

CATH. Do I like the *table*?

PHIL. Yes. Do you like the table?

Pause.

CATH. Look, we've got to *clean* the place . . .

PHIL. No, this is important.

Pause.

CATH. You want me to tell you truthfully whether I like the table?

PHIL. I want you to tell me truthfully whether you like the table.

Pause. She looks at it.

CATH. I don't know whether I like the table.

PHIL. You don't know whether you like the table?

CATH. What do you want me to say?

PHIL. I want you to say what you want to say.

CATH. It's a table.

PHIL. Oh. Right. Thank you.

CATH. Right?

PHIL. Right. It's a table.

They pick the table up and carry it out.

CATH (*off*). Mind!

PHIL (*off*). What?

A splintering sound, off.

CATH (*off*). I said Mind!

PHIL (*off*). What does it matter?

They reappear.

It's only a table. Chairs?

CATH *You* take the chairs.

She gives him the two original chairs.

PHIL. And as far as you're concerned they're just . . . chairs?

CATH. Yes. Throw *them* down the stairs as well.

He takes the chairs out.

Anyway, you're the one who doesn't like the chairs.

He comes back.

PHIL *I* don't like the chairs?

CATH. You don't like Eric's chair.

She hands it to him.

PHIL. I don't like Eric's chair?

CATH. Well, you don't.

PHIL. I sit on it!

CATH. You never *did* like it.

PHIL. When didn't I like it?

CATH. You've forgotten.

PHIL. I haven't forgotten.

CATH. You never remember when you've changed your mind about something.

PHIL. I haven't changed my mind.

CATH. You're always changing your mind.

PHIL. What?

She takes the chair out of his hands and puts it outside.

CATH (*off*). You didn't like this place for a start.

PHIL. What do you mean, I didn't like this place?

CATH (*off*). You walked through this door . . .

She comes in.

You took one look round . . .

She looks round. The room is now almost as empty as when they first saw it.

And you said, no.

PHIL. No, I didn't.

CATH. You said it twice. You said it three times. 'No. No. No!'

PHIL. I said What do you think?

CATH. You were standing here. I remember.

PHIL. I was standing *here*.

CATH. 'No. No. No.'

PHIL. 'What do you think?'

CATH. 'No. No. No.' We told Pat we didn't want it!

PHIL. 'What do you think?' That's what I said! I was standing exactly *here*!

CATH. Yes, and what did *I* say?

PHIL. What did *you* say? I'll tell you what you said. You said No. No, no, no.

CATH. I said What do *you* think?

PHIL. I said Yes.

CATH. You said No.

PHIL. I said Yes.

CATH. All right, you said Yes.

She pulls out the vacuum-cleaner from behind the curtain, and hands it to him while she plugs it in.

PHIL. I did.

CATH. Yes.

PHIL. Yes.

CATH. Yes!

He stands there, holding the vacuum-cleaner.

PHIL. What I said was, we ought to think carefully about it, because it was going to be part of our life. Which it *was*. It *was* part of our life.

CATH. Switch it on, then. Or are we *taking* the dust?

PHIL *Taking* the dust?

CATH. I don't like the dust? What am I trying to say? I used to like the dust. When did I stop liking the dust?

PHIL *I'm* not the one who's changed.

CATH *The* dust? *Our* dust. Give me that.

She takes the vacuum-cleaner, switches on and starts to clean the room. She finds the alarm clock on the floor as she works, and shifts it nearer the other remaining items.

PHIL *(shouts over the noise)*. *I'll* do it!

CATH *(shouts)*. You do the things!

PHIL. I said *I'll* do it!

CATH. Do the *things*!

He picks up the remaining items.

Not *that* thing! That's for last!

He dumps an open floppy bag back on the floor. It's exactly where she is going to vacuum.

Not there!

He takes the other things out. She moves the floppy bag in exasperation. It covers up the alarm clock.

No, you *haven't* changed.

He comes back in.

PHIL. What?

CATH. You still contradict everything I say.

PHIL. *I* contradict?

CATH. I say yes, you say no. I say do, you say don't.

PHIL. I say I said yes, you say I said no. I say I'll do that, you say No you won't.

Enter PAT, *unnoticed in the noise and argument.*

CATH. You wouldn't know what you thought if I didn't say the opposite.

PHIL. You wouldn't know what *you* thought if I didn't say something for you to say the opposite to.

PAT *finds the toy dog, and holds it up.*

CATH. I often think you hate me.

PHIL. Yes. Sometimes.

CATH *switches off the vacuum-cleaner.*

CATH. You don't!

PHIL. You see?

CATH. What?

PHIL. Who's contradicting who?

PAT. There's always one thing gets left behind.

CATH. Oh, Pat.

PAT. Don't forget this. You're going to be needing toys now.

She puts the dog down near the floppy bag.

CATH. Oh, Pat! We're going to miss you.

PAT. No, you're not. You'll never think about me again.

PAT *unplugs the vacuum-cleaner and winds up the cord.*

CATH. We will!

PHIL. We'll come and see you!

PAT. You won't, you know. You've gone? You've gone. Last you'll see of me – last I'll see of you. And I'll tell you something else, my loves. *I'm* not going to miss *you*. You walk out that door and you've walked off the face of the earth as far as I'm concerned. Who cares? See if *I* mind.

She goes out carrying the vacuum-cleaner, PHIL *goes to follow her.* CATH *stops him.*

CATH *Do* you?

PHIL. What?

CATH. Hate me?

PHIL. Oh – no.

CATH. You do.

PHIL. And there you go! I say I don't. You say I do.

CATH. You said you did.

PHIL. I didn't!

CATH. You did!

PHIL. *You* said I did!

CATH. Yes. Well . . .

PHIL. Come on.

CATH. All the same, you don't really . . .

PHIL. Don't really what? Oh, no!

CATH. No?

PHIL. Yes!

CATH. You don't.

PHIL. I do! How many times?

CATH. Yes . . .

PHIL. Yes!

They start to go, then CATH *stops and looks round the room. It is completely empty except for the floppy bag.*

Now what's the matter?

CATH. Nothing. Just . . .

PHIL. What?

She opens the kitchenette.

CATH. That cooker could have done with a bit more work.

He looks into the bathroom.

PHIL. So could the bath.

CATH. Yes. Well . . .

He closes the bathroom.

PHIL. What are we going to forget?

CATH. What do you mean?

PHIL. Always one thing.

CATH. Oh . . .

She looks round, sees the toy dog and picks it up.

PHIL. Nearly. So, what do you think? Yes or no?

CATH. What?

PHIL. Take it? This place?

CATH. Oh . . .

She drops the dog into the floppy bag and looks round.

Yes.

PHIL. Yes?

CATH. Yes!

PHIL. Yes.

He opens the door. She stands taking a last look round.

What?

CATH. Oh . . . Nothing. Everything . . .

She quickly goes out. He takes one last look himself.

PHIL. We'll never see it again.

He goes out and closes the door behind them. A moment later it opens again, and she runs back in, irritated.

CATH. What are you doing?

She picks up the floppy bag. He reappears in the doorway.

PHIL. What am *I* doing?

CATH. You left it there!

PHIL *I* left it there? *We* left it there . . .!

By this time they are outside again, and closing the door. The lights fade, leaving only the alarm-clock that was underneath the bag illuminated. It ticks slowly on.

Curtain.